DINOSAUR SAMURAI

"What's going on?" Peter asked. "What did he say?"

"Lord Akira said that it was unfortunate that you came snooping around here. It was most unfortunate that you recognized him."

"I was only looking for Katsu," Peter said quickly, realizing that suddenly he was in big trouble. "I can see he's not here. I'll be going now."

Akira spat a few more words in Japanese. Mundo smiled, exposing his long, glittering fangs.

"I'm afraid that's not possible."

He grabbed Peter's arm. Peter tried to shake him off, but the ape was a lot stronger. He kicked out and had the satisfaction of landing a solid blow on Mundo's shin. Mundo winced, but he held on.

Peter drew his foot back to kick again, then something crashed on the back of his head. He tried to shake off the effects of the blow, but couldn't. His knees went rubbery as he lost the strength in his legs and slumped to the stable floor, unconscious.

R A Y   B R A D B U R Y
P R E S E N T S

DINOSAUR
SAMURAI

Ray Bradbury's Dinosaur Series #1
DINOSAUR WORLD
by Stephen Leigh, illustrated by Wayne D. Barlowe

Ray Bradbury's Dinosaur Series #2
DINOSAUR PLANET
by Stephen Leigh, illustrated by John Paul Genzo

Ray Bradbury's Dinosaur Series #3
DINOSAUR SAMURAI
by Stephen Leigh and John J. Miller,
illustrated by Brian Franczak

Ray Bradbury's Dinosaur Series #4
DINOSAUR WARRIORS
by Stephen Leigh, illustrated by Nicholas Jainschigg

Ray Bradbury's Dinosaur Series #5
DINOSAUR EMPIRE
by Stephen Leigh and John J. Miller,
illustrated by Nicholas Jainschigg and Cortney Skinner

Ray Bradbury's Dinosaur Series #6
DINOSAUR CONQUEST
by Stephen Leigh, illustrated by Cortney Skinner

TIME SAFARI, INC.
SAFARIS TO ANY YEAR IN THE PAST.
You name the animal. We take you there.

R A Y   B R A D B U R Y
P R E S E N T S

DINOSAUR SAMURAI

A NOVEL BY
STEPHEN LEIGH AND
JOHN J. MILLER

Illustrated by
Brian Franczak

A Byron Preiss Book

J. T. Colby & Company, Inc.
Purveyors of Time Travel Instruments and Accessories™

J. T. Colby & Company, Inc.
Purveyors of Time Travel Instruments and Accessories™

Dinosaur Samurai

"Time Safari, Inc." is a trademark of
Byron Preiss Visual Publications.

Library of Congress Cataloging-in-Publication Data
Leigh, Stephen.
Miller, John J.
Ray Bradbury Presents Dinosaur Samurai.
        (Ray Bradbury Presents) "A Byron Preiss Visual
Publications book."
p. cm.
        [1. Science Fiction—Time Travel. 2. Fiction—Science
Fiction—Adventure. 3.] I. Franczak, Brian iII. II. Title. III.
Series: Ray Bradbury Presents.

J. T. Colby & Company, Inc.
Purveyors of Time Travel Instruments and Accessories™

Manhanset House
Dering Harbor, New York 11965-0342
bricktower@aol.com
bricktowerpress.com

ISBN: 978-1-59687-583-8
January 2019

To Mom,
with love and thanks for buying that book
with dinosaurs on the cover in Whalen's drugstore
all those years ago

Table of Contents

1

Lost on a Lost World

Peter Finnigan was hungry. And dirty. And tired. He enjoyed camping when he had a house to come back to, a house with a comfortable bed, a hot shower, and a refrigerator full of food. Now, trapped in a timeline on a world where humanity had never evolved, all he had was a cave with a pile of leaves, a cold stream, and a forest stocked with food that he had to stalk, capture, and cook himself.

The forest was an odd place, loaded with unfamiliar plants and animals Peter had never seen before. There were a few real trees, evergreens of some kind, but no trees with leaves. Other plants masqueraded as trees, but were actually ferns or overgrown shrubs. Mammals were furry skittering things skulking around the huge ferns or scampering through the branches above. None were bigger than a rat.

Reptiles ruled this world.

Peter crouched near a club-shaped cycad that looked like a rough-barked palm tree, checking the crude snare that he and Eckels, his fellow time traveler, had set the day before. It had been sprung, but had failed to hold whatever had set it off. Peter sat back on his heels, frowning.

"Why Eckels?" he asked himself aloud. "Why couldn't I have been marooned with Travis? He's the big hunter. I'll bet he could live off this land, easy. Instead I get stuck with the rich guy who probably wouldn't even know how to warm up a microwave dinner. If we had a microwave dinner. Or a microwave."

Peter stood up with a sigh, rubbing his rumbling stomach. It hadn't even been this bad when he'd been a captive of the Mutata. At least then he and Jennifer Mason, the girl he'd got lost with, had been fed regularly by the intelligent reptiles native to this weird world.

The next snare was off the trail to the left, in front of a dead evergreen whose trunk leaned to the ground. Peter started toward it, then stopped.

Someone, or something, was coming down the trail toward him. Several somethings, in fact. He could hear them thrashing through the shrubs that bordered and overhung the path. Eckels wouldn't make that much noise. He wasn't big enough, by far. The intruders had to be something else. Mutata—or worse, Gairk.

The Mutata might be big lizards, but at least you could sort of talk to them. They were dangerous, sure, but they were vegetarians. The Gairk, though, were predators through and through. Peter knew that he and Eckels, and probably even Jennifer, were under a Gairk death sentence. The Gairk, like most of the Mutata, believed the coming of humans portended the destruction of their world. They thought they could save their world by eliminating the humans—and the Gairk, ugly bundles of reflexes lashed together by tough muscle and scaled skin, didn't stop to argue about their beliefs.

Peter stood in the middle of the path, trying to decide what to do. He was unarmed. Eckels had a rifle, but he kept it stashed in the cave and never let Peter use it. Both races of reptiles were technologically primitive, but a stone spear could kill you just as dead as a bullet. Peter was strong and athletic, but no human was a physical match for either the Mutata or the Gairk. Both species had retained the teeth, claws, and armor of their less intelligent ancestors.

Peter decided to run, to stick to the trail and try to make it back to the cave. It was too dangerous to attempt a shortcut through the forest, too easy to trip over a root or get lost and end up running in circles.

Peter turned, but it was too late. Two dinosaurs came around the curve in the trail and stared at him with unblinking eyes. He stared back, his heart sinking.

They were Gairk.

Nearly ten feet tall, they stood on powerful hind legs, their long, graceful tails held stiffly behind them to help them keep their balance. Their forearms looked short and weak compared to their powerful hind-limbs, but in reality they were larger and stronger than Peter's arms. Crude helmets of beaten copper sat atop their bald heads like ridiculous salad bowls and they wore copper armor plates on their chests. Their tails were banded with tanned lizard-skin straps decorated with nodules of raw ore and they carried wooden clubs studded with razor-sharp obsidian blades that gleamed like black glass.

Their faces were frighteningly inhuman. Peter had to remind himself that these creatures were as intelligent as he. Their jaws full of the sharply pointed teeth of the carnivore, they were the supreme warriors of the dinosaur world. Their motto was attack first and ask questions later. Peter knew that he couldn't even contemplate negotiating with them or fighting them.

They shrieked at Peter in a language that consisted mainly of roars, snorts, and coughs, with a few consonants thrown in. He didn't try to decipher what they were saying. He took off down the trail.

Peter was a star athlete with great pride in his accomplishments on the track and gridiron. But this chase was different. He wasn't trying to get away from a ball-hungry tackler. He was running for his life. And the things chasing him could really move.

He started with a sixty-yard lead on his pursuers. He risked a glance over his shoulder and saw that the Gairk had halved the distance between them in the first ten seconds of the chase. *I've never had to outrun a defensive end who was* that *fast,* Peter thought. Sweat beaded his forehead from fear and exertion both. He knew in his heart, now pounding like a beaten drum in his heaving chest, that he couldn't win this race.

What to do? he asked himself with a silent sob. *What to do? What to do?*

The forest was quiet. The still, humid air seemed to clog Peter's lungs. It was as if everything had stopped to watch this race to the death, a race Peter was sure he was going to lose.

The Gairk were gaining on him. He could hear their clawed feet thudding on the loose forest loam, closer and closer. The skin between his shoulder blades crawled as he imagined their claws dragging him down, pinning him to the ground like a helpless, hopeless insect. He could smell their thick, reptilian musk; he could hear their shuddering breathing. Right on his heels a Gairk roared in triumph and he suddenly knew what he had to do.

Peter leapt, hurling himself at a low-hanging branch of a conifer that stuck out over the forest trail. The branch was maybe nine feet off the ground, but Peter grabbed it with both hands. His right hand slipped, but somehow he managed to catch hold again. He let his momentum carry him forward in a great arc and he hooked his right leg around a higher branch and hung upside down for a moment like a huge, panting sloth.

The Gairk had blundered past the tree and were just now stumbling to a halt. Though it was normally impossible to read their alien features, Peter felt certain he saw astonishment and sudden rage on their reptilian faces. One of them did a ferocious, stamping dance, shaking his club and bellowing like an angry bull.

Peter knew that he wasn't safe yet. He took a shuddering breath, his grateful lungs drinking in the oxygen-rich air, then pulled himself up to a standing position on the thick branch hanging over the trail. He looked down to see one of the Gairk leap up and swing his club at the branch. The lizard couldn't jump very high—but was taller than Peter had realized. Peter leapt for the next branch, and hauled himself further into the tree just as a blow from the Gairk's club smashed the limb he'd been standing on.

Finally he was out of their reach. Finally he was safe. Struck by a wave of relief that brought on an attack of giddiness, he made a face at his tormentors.

"Can't climb trees, can you, you lousy lizards!"

One of the Gairk drew his arm back. Peter flinched and pulled back just as the dinosaur flung his club. Tree branches deflected the weapon, then caught it. For a moment Peter considered trying to retrieve it for his own use, but decided not to. The other Gairk was eyeing him closely, his arm cocked and ready. It would be foolish, Peter decided, to do anything to make himself a better target.

The conifer had thick, sturdy branches. Peter climbed higher, stopping when he was about thirty feet off the ground. The Gairk stood under his tree, craning their necks to get a good look at him and grumbling to themselves in their guttural language. They weren't climbers. They weren't even trying to follow him.

Peter turned around slowly, surveying the forest from his perch. The sun was throwing long bars of dusty light through the overlapping branches of the trees. It would soon be night and Peter could move without the Gairk seeing him. He just had to keep quiet.

He studied the branches of a neighboring tree very carefully. He wasn't free of the hunters just yet. It wouldn't do to fall and land at their feet.

"Now exactly how," Peter asked himself, "did Tarzan do this tree-swinging bit?"

Very carefully he selected a pair of interlocking branches and gingerly moved from his tree to the next.

Aaron Cofield watched carefully as Travis set the time machine down on the bit of temporal roadway that floated a few inches above the ground. Aaron wasn't an expert on running a time machine yet, but he was getting there. The computer interface was a snap and the actual controls hardly more complicated than those of a car.

Aaron knew that he and Travis were in for some dangerous times. It would be better if both knew how to run the machine in case Travis, the cross-temporal safari guide and time machine pilot, was incapacitated—or worse. Even now Aaron worried about his companion. He suspected that Travis was more seriously injured than either one of them would like to believe. Between the cough and the limp and the way he'd sometimes stop and hold his side . . .

"Well," Travis said with a tired sigh. "Here we are."

"Wherever here is," the third member of their party said sarcastically.

"Looks better than where you came from, bud," Travis replied.

"My name's Mundo, not bud."

Actually, his name wasn't even Mundo. He hadn't had a name, or even a body, when he'd first met Aaron and Travis. Mundo had been a world-spirit, an entity who was part of everything in his home timeline. He'd simply taken over the body of the apelike creature he now inhabited to make it easier to interact with his new acquaintances. Mundo had joined Aaron and Travis on a whim and now was just as lost and just as desperate to find his home timeline.

Aaron didn't particularly trust the creature. Mundo was an utterly alien, utterly self-absorbed being who lacked normal human emotion. Aaron didn't trust him, but he and Travis were stuck with him.

"Let's explore," Aaron suggested. "Grandpa Carl should be around here somewhere. He can't be too far ahead of us." Aaron's grandfather had mistakenly entered this time-line looking for Aaron. Now they were on his trail.

Travis nodded and worked the controls. The time machine slipped down off the temporal roadway until it hovered just above the soft forest loam. Aaron peered through the front viewscreen, looking for clues to both his grandfather's whereabouts and the identity of their new temporal location. The sun was getting ready to set. Its light was the soft golden green of dusk. They were in a clearing surrounded by evergreens, cycads, and huge ferns. Aaron could see little besides the greenery, but they seemed to be on a slope with the summit of a ridge towering close above them.

"Looks like we're still in the Mesozoic," Aaron said thoughtfully, "but maybe a later period. The Jurassic?"

Travis nodded in agreement. "Too many flowering plants for the early Mesozoic. Listen, I want to try something. Maybe we can reach one of our HomeTimes from here. Let's try a short hop UpTime."

Aaron felt the outline of the IC card, the temporal circuitry governor, in his shirt pocket. Travis had given it to him to hold with the warning that the fuel needed for temporal jumps was dangerously low. They couldn't afford to take useless trips in time. Still, this timestream might lead to Travis's particular future, or Mundo's. Or maybe even his own.

"You think there's still enough juice for three or four jumps?"

Travis shrugged. "Probably. Maybe. I can't make any promises."

"Okay," Aaron said slowly. "Let's try 1992."

"What?" Mundo asked angrily. "What about me? Is finding your own HomeTimes the only important thing we have to do? What about getting me back home?"

Aaron glanced at the creature. His voice, the way he talked, his precise words and phrases were becoming more and more human. It was as if being with them for the past few days was tuning him in to the way human minds worked and to the way humans expressed themselves. Aaron didn't know if this was good or bad, but it showed that Mundo was adaptable. Or maybe sly was a better word.

Travis sighed tiredly and rubbed his lean, tanned face. "You're right. We have to get you home, too. We'll try . . ."

Travis let his voice dwindle and shrugged resignedly. Aaron knew that the temporal guide was gradually losing all hope of ever finding the way out of the mess in which they had found themselves. They had to achieve some success, however small, or Travis might fly into one of his all-consuming rages and do something dangerous. Aaron still remembered how crazy Travis had acted on Mundo's world. He didn't want that to happen again.

"This reality might be home for any of us," Aaron said as encouragingly as he could. "Let's do it."

He slid under the panel and inserted the IC into its socket. Travis set the controls and looked at Aaron before thumbing the final switch. There was misery and near-hopelessness in his eyes. Aaron gave him the best smile he could manage and nodded decisively. Travis punched the button.

"Activating . . ." the machine's computer said in its sexless voice. The temporal engines began their high whine and abruptly shut off. "Calibration error," the computer told them. "We are currently in HomeTime."

All the muscle seemed to go out of Travis's body. He slumped bonelessly in his seat, his eyes smoldering darkly under the ridge of his brow.

"Just like last time," he said flatly. "This is a different timeline altogether. This is HomeTime for us now. We might as well give up."

"Travis," Aaron said, "come on. We still have to find my grandfather. I *need* you."

Travis shook him off. "Nothing we can do will do any good," he muttered despairingly.

Aaron mulled over the implications of what had just happened. This, he realized, not necessarily bad news. Sure, they were in a new timeline, but Aaron wasn't quite sure what that meant in the long run. Unfortunately Travis was too far gone at the moment to discuss things and Mundo was useless in situations like this. Aaron looked at Travis. He was staring into space and muttering to himself between clenched teeth. Aaron knew that he had to get Travis out of his dismal mood. He had to get him moving and functioning again.

"Look," Aaron said, "we're certainly doing no good sitting around here. Let's go out and explore. Maybe we can find my grandfather. Maybe," Aaron said, suddenly inspired, "Eckels is somewhere in this world."

Travis's eyes focused at the mention of Eckels's name.

Eckels had caused the temporal disaster in which they had all got lost. A client of Travis's temporal safari firm, Eckels had lost his courage at the sight of a Tyrannosaurus rex, broken, run, and stolen a time machine, causing a temporal paradox that had blown he roadway into pieces. The explosion had either created or simply opened the way into the multiple alternate realities in which Eckels, Travis, Aaron, Mundo, Carl—and Aaron's friends Peter and Jennifer—were lost.

Travis rose from his chair, turned, and looked back at Aaron.

"Let's go," he said, grabbing the rifle from where it hung on the weapons rack. "Let's find Eckels." Then, just a touch too late to make his words sound entirely sincere: "And your grandfather, too, of course."

Peter and Eckels had only been gone a few weeks, but Jennifer Mason already missed their companionship. It was difficult to be all alone among an utterly alien race, even if the race was as fascinating as the Mutata.

Over the last month Jennifer had made great strides with the Mutata language, mastering it as completely as any human could. Humans lacked the proper physical equipment to vocalize the hoots, bleats, and nasal blatts that were all important parts of the Mutata vocabulary, but she'd managed to pick up many of the intricacies of the dinosaurs' complicated body language that gave subtle meaning and rich texture to their spoken words. The third part of their language—the olfactory element—continued to be a problem. Jennifer was unable consciously to control her odor, so she was mute in this facet of their tongue. That bothered the Mutata, even friendly ones like SStragh and Raajek. The Mutata knew only one way of doing things. They weren't favorably disposed to change, basing their entire life on what they called the OColihi, the Ancient Path.

SStragh was one of the few Mutata who attempted to understand Jennifer. As near as any dinosaur could come to the concept, SStragh was a friend.

"You have the OColihi to guide your lives," Jennifer said as they shared a meal of fruits and vegetables while reclining on couches like feasting Romans in SStragh's living space. The Mutata didn't have individual dwelling places, but specific areas within the hivelike structure of their village were set aside for specific individuals. SStragh's area was near the compound's edge since she was something of an outsider among her tribe. She was one of the few to champion the cause of Jennifer and the other humans. Worse, before Jennifer and the others had arrived on her world, SStragh had been a pupil of Raajek, the outcast OTsio, or teacher, who had advocated changing the OColihi. Such a thought was considered worse than blasphemy by most Mutata.

"And you don't, Jhenini." SStragh's body language indicated that her words were more of a statement than a question.

Jennifer nodded as she bit into a tangy, citrusy thing that tasted like an orange with a cinnamon underflavor. They'd had this discussion before, sometimes with Raajek present. SStragh had come to the point where she could intellectually accept the fact that the humans didn't have a rigidly codified set of rules and regulations totally running their lives. But she still didn't really believe it in her reptilian heart.

"We call our path . . ." Jennifer ran through her Mutata vocabulary and was astonished that she couldn't find the word she was searching for. She used the English word instead, " . . . *laws* that are decided upon by the majority of the people in our . . . tribe. Most people obey them, but some do not. In fact, there are some laws that many people disobey. If enough people dislike a law, then we change it."

SStragh's spinal crest rose, showing her excitement. "You change your . . . *luwsss* . . ." she stumbled over the word " . . . like the OColihi needs to be changed."

"My people find change less threatening than your people. Some of my people, anyway."

"The Mutata will not stray from the OColihi, even if . . . even if it would be best to."

Jennifer had the feeling that SStragh had started to say "even if the OColihi is wrong," but couldn't bring herself to speak such blasphemy aloud.

"We must follow what the OColi tells us is the Path," SStragh finished.

Jennifer suddenly had a sense of where this was leading.

"I can't help you find Peter and Eckels," she told SStragh. "I won't help you kill them."

"The OColi has ordered it," SStragh said. "That is why Raajek cannot be with us now. The OColi has forbidden her to see you until Peeitah and Eikels are found. I was ordered to tell you this."

The OColi was the oldest of the Mutata, and their leader. He believed that the Dreaming Storms wracking the Mutatas' valley were caused by the humans. Jennifer knew that in a sense this was true. Eckels's actions had caused the sections of temporal roadway—what the Mutata and their cousins the Gairk called the Floating Stones—to appear in the valley. Jennifer suspected that the storms, which caused weird fragments of landscape to appear and then vanish like flickering dreams, were a by-product of the accident. But sacrificing Peter and Eckels to the All-Ancestor was not going to mend things.

"You told me you and Peeitah found Eikels's cave," SStragh said. "You have been there before—that is what you told me."

"You think that's where they've gone? To the cave?"

"That is what the OColi believes."

Jennifer shook her head. "I . . . I can't take you there, SStragh. Peter and I stumbled across it, and I really don't remember . . ." She stopped, uncomfortable with the lie. "Even if I knew the way, I couldn't let the OColi and Frraghi have them."

"I try to understand," SStragh said. She popped half a dozen of the cinnamon apples into her mouth, ground her massive jaws together, and swallowed. "It may not be for the Mutata, after all, to send Peeitah and Eikels to the All-Ancestor."

"What do you mean?" Jennifer asked.

SStragh looked at her, her face as unreadable as ever. "Remember what the Gairk Envoy Klaido has declared. The Gairk hunt them, too," she said, "and when they catch them they will kill them."

2

Nightfall

It was dark by the time Peter reached the cave he shared with Eckels. He climbed to the ground a few hundred yards from the entrance, first checking to make sure he hadn't been followed by the Gairk before dropping out of the tree.

The night breezes were cool enough to make Peter wish he was wearing something heavier than a frayed pair of jeans and a ragged T-shirt. There were a few small skins in the cave, but neither he nor Eckels had advanced far enough in the art of tanning to make garments out of them. There weren't very many furred animals in this world and the ones that did exist were small and difficult to catch. Making a shirt out of their skins would be like making a hamster-skin coat. It wasn't impossible, but you would need a whole lot of hamsters.

Bare limestone outcroppings stood out starkly on the hillside like bones from the scavenged corpse of a giant. The entrance to the cave was high on the slope, guarded by several huge boulders. Peter went past the boulders, slithered down a short, steep incline, and entered the cave mouth. Even at the entrance he could smell the smoke of the cook fire and feel the coolness of the air, damp with the odors of earth and rock.

The entrance was actually a narrow, cramped passage that gave Peter the creeps every time he traversed it. Living in a cave was not exactly the best thing for his claustrophobia, but he had little choice in the matter. The cave was a necessary refuge against the dangers of the dinosaur world.

The darkness didn't help either. It was easy for Peter to make his way through the corridor during the daytime, when sunlight filtered through the cracks in the ceiling, providing enough light so that he didn't bump into the walls where the tunnel jigged and jagged. Peter had been in and out of the cave dozens of times since he and Eckels had escaped from the Mutata village. He knew the way pretty well, but not perfectly. It was more difficult at night. He went slowly, wincing whenever he barked his shins or stubbed his toes on the rocks that littered the floor.

Eckels was sitting cross-legged before the fire, warming himself as he watched the contents of the crude clay cook pot bubble away. He looked up when Peter entered the small chamber.

"Where've you been?" he asked, stirring the simmering pot with a handy stick.

"Up a tree," Peter said with a sigh. He collapsed next to the fire and held his hands out to warm. "What's cooking?"

"Rat and lizard stew," Eckels said briefly. He looked at Peter and cocked an eyebrow. "I see you didn't bring anything to contribute."

"I was lucky to get away myself," Peter protested. "Those damn lizards almost had me."

"Mutata?" Eckels asked with disinterest.

"Worse. Gairk. I had to climb a tree to get away from them."

Eckels looked up from the pot, interest in his eyes for the first time. "So the Gairk are hunting us?" His gaze suddenly narrowed. "Are you sure you got away from them?"

"Sure I'm sure."

Peter leaned forward to sniff at the boiling pot. It didn't smell particularly appetizing, but he was really hungry. After a couple of weeks on the dinosaur world Peter had learned to eat anything that wasn't moving. If he stayed much longer, even that requirement might go out the window.

Eckels grabbed Peter's arm, his clawlike fingers digging into Peter's biceps. Eckels wasn't a large man—Peter was bigger and more muscular—but his intensity gave him a strength that Peter couldn't match.

"You'd better make sure," he hissed at Peter. "The Gairk are master hunters, not like those plant-eating Mutata. They can smell meat a mile away. And they know what *you* smell like, I can guarantee that. I wouldn't like it very much if you led them to my cave."

Peter tried to pull away, but he couldn't break Eckels's grip.

"Hey, let go," he complained. "You're hurting."

Eckels continued to glare.

"Okay, okay," Peter said. "I know I shook them, but I'll go check if you want."

"I want."

"Okay."

Eckels let him go. Peter stood, rubbing the marks Eckels's fingers had left on his arm.

"Can I at least have the rifle?" Peter asked.

Eckels reached out to where the weapon leaned against the tree stump that served as their table. He grabbed it by the barrel and put it across his lap.

"The rifle's mine."

"Yeah, right. It seems to me it was originally Travis's. You were just as surprised as me to find it stashed here."

Eckels just stared at him.

"C'mon, Eckels," Peter persisted. "In case the Gairk are out there."

Eckels looked down and stirred the cook pot. End of conversation, Peter decided. What a great guy to have as a boon companion. Peter stood and went over to where they had stockpiled a number of crude torches against the cave wall. He selected one and lighted it at the camp-fire, but Eckels continued to ignore him.

"Wish he'd lighten up a little," Peter grumbled as he started up the corridor. "Does he think I *want* to be here? I didn't want anything to do with this whole thing, anyway. It was all Jennifer's fault. Jennifer's and Aaron's."

Peter sighed aloud. Jennifer Mason had been his girl—at least he'd considered her his girl—before she'd taken up with Aaron Cofield. Aaron had been his best friend. Maybe he hadn't been sure about Jennifer before she started going with Aaron, but he knew now that he wanted her back. He couldn't see why in the world she preferred Aaron to him. Aaron was a good enough guy, though he'd become something of a book geek in the last few years, but—

Peter reached the end of the corridor and stuck his head out of the entrance flanked by the precariously piled boulders.

Nothing. Just as he'd thought. Nothing but the cool night air . . . Which smelled kind of funny . . .

He peered around one of the boulders and found himself face to face with a Gairk, who was peering around from the other side.

"Holy—" Peter began.

The Gairk rose to its full height, opened its huge, dagger-toothed mouth, and roared.

Peter gagged, frozen by the awful nearness of the killing machine. He was so close that he could see the strips of flesh from the Gairk's last meal clinging to its yellow teeth. The reptile's fetid breath crawled into Peter's nostrils and down his throat.

The Gairk drew back to strike, lifting its obsidian-edged club high. But the creature was slow, so lethargic in the cool night air that Peter had a chance to recover his wits. He scuttled backward as the club began its savage descent. The blow would have pulped his head like a watermelon tossed out of a ten-story building, but just missed.

The club whistled past Peter's face and he threw his torch at the Gairk, then dropped to his hands and knees and crawled away as fast as he could. The Gairk roared again and lunged after him, but the space between the boulders was too narrow. The dinosaur couldn't push his bulk between the stones. Peter hoped they were also too large for the Gairk's inhuman strength to move.

Once inside the passageway Peter stood and hurried as quickly as he dared into the darkness. His breath came in quick pants as his natural claustrophobia combined with the fear and adrenaline rush brought on by his unexpected meeting with the Gairk.

He was almost crying as he burst into the small chamber where he and Eckels lived. Eckels was drinking stew from one of their crude ceramic cups, the rifle close at hand. He raised his eyebrows at Peter's sudden entrance.

"I hate this place!" Peter exploded. "I want to get out of here! I want to go home!"

"Don't we all," Eckels said. "I heard your friend roaring out there. He followed you to our lair, didn't he?"

Peter nodded miserably. "What are we going to do now?"

Eckels finished the stew and put the bowl down. "We can't stay here." He looked around the cave. "I hate to leave such stellar accommodations."

"The thing can't get in after us," Peter said. "The entrance is too small—"

Eckels shook his head. "You forget that these lizards are intelligent. They'll find a way—or get their cousins the Mutata to come in after us. They'd be able to squeeze through the passageway."

"Then what do we do?" Peter asked plaintively.

"We leave. Now's the best time, before they become fully active in the morning." Eckels stood up. "I don't suppose you noticed how many Gairk were waiting for us?"

"I didn't have time to take a census!" Peter snapped.

"No, I don't suppose you did. I guess that means we have to go out the hard way."

"What's that?" Peter asked.

"I hope you're not afraid of small, enclosed spaces," Eckels said.

Peter swallowed hard.

"On second thought," Travis said, "it's going to be dark soon. Maybe we should hole up in the time machine for the night."

"We went through the portal no more than ten or fifteen minutes after Grandpa Carl," Aaron said anxiously. "He's probably still close by. Now's our best chance to find him, before he wanders off somewhere."

"Will it be dangerous?" Mundo asked. Since becoming trapped in a mortal body far from his own timestream, Mundo had displayed a well-developed sense of caution.

"Living is dangerous," Travis said unsympathetically. "Get used to it."

"It shouldn't be too bad, even in the dark," Aaron added reassuringly. "We have lights. Travis has his rifle."

"Maybe I should stay behind and guard the time machine," Mundo said.

Travis and Aaron exchanged doubtful glances. Aaron knew what Travis was thinking. Mundo was a strange creature who was just beginning to understand what it meant to have a single, permanent body. He had nothing approaching human emotions. Aaron wouldn't put it past him to try something underhanded if left alone with the time machine . . . like making a desperate, useless attempt to find his home timeline by himself.

"Noooo," Aaron said slowly. "I figure that it'd be more dangerous to split our forces. Much more dangerous. Especially for the one who was left alone. Wouldn't you say so, Travis?"

"Sure," Travis deadpanned. "But if you're *volunteering* for this dangerous job—"

"No, no," Mundo broke in hastily. "Aaron is right. We shouldn't split up. I'll go with you."

Aaron felt a twinge of guilt at manipulating Mundo— but only a little twinge. Their lives depended on working together. If Mundo needed a nudge every now and then to be a good team player, Aaron would nudge him.

In fact, the image of Mundo careening wildly though time made Aaron decidedly nervous. Aaron waited until Travis found the hand lamps in the tool locker and took Mundo outside, then he slipped under the control panel and again removed the IC card from its socket. He stashed it in a nest of wires in another part of the circuitry, just in case.

He stood, brushed his pants off, and joined the others outside as darkness descended on the world.

SStragh couldn't think or move normally in the coolness of the night, but the Mutatas' susceptibility to cold was at the heart of Jennifer's plan. Night was the safest time to look for Peter and Eckels. No other Mutata would interfere, since none could conceive of such a scheme. Nocturnal excursions went against the grain of the OColihi, and she and SStragh would be free from the prying eyes of Frraghi and his faction. Jennifer knew she could find the cave again, though she hadn't admitted that to SStragh yet.

Jennifer wasn't sure what she would do once they found Peter and Eckels. SStragh was as obedient to the direct orders of the OColi as any Mutata. She figured that SStragh intended for the two humans to throw themselves on the uncertain mercy of the OColi. She let SStragh believe that this was her intention as well.

But Jennifer was certain that Peter and Eckels would be killed if they returned to the Mutata village, almost as certainly as they'd be killed if the Gairk found them. She didn't know what to do yet, but she'd think of something when the time came. She did know, though, that she needed to see them again. She needed to talk to her own kind. The last few weeks had been horribly lonely.

The night was cool, but not uncomfortable as long as they kept moving. The chill air was harder on SStragh. Her physiology was somewhere between the cold-bloodedness of reptiles and the warm-bloodedness of mammals. She could function without the warmth of the sun, but it took conscious willpower for her to act and both her mental and physical reactions were slower than normal.

SStragh followed Jennifer uncomplainingly as she led the way through the forest trails. It had been weeks since Jennifer—in the company of Raajek and SStragh—had stumbled across the location of Eckels's cave very near where she'd found the body of Aaron's grandfather. That had been in the daytime. Jennifer was discovering that it was difficult to find her way back. At night the trees all looked alike and there were few land-marks in the dark forest.

She stopped at a place where the trail forked, uncertain which direction to take.

"Which way, Jhenini?" SStragh asked in a slow, almost pained voice. Jennifer had the feeling that if SStragh were capable of shivering, her teeth would be chattering right now. They couldn't waste time standing around. SStragh couldn't take too much of it. She would slow down even more and become totally torpid until warmed by the morning sun.

"This way—I think." She started to go down the right-hand fork, then hesitated. The gigantic cycad standing near the trail's left fork looked familiar. Was that the way?

She was standing there, indecisive, when she heard the sound of a large body stomping toward them on the trail. She glanced up at SStragh, but was unable to read her companion's reptilian expression.

SStragh had heard it, too. "Something is coming," she said. "Something bigger than a Mutata."

"Gairk?" Jennifer asked. She had no great desire to meet one of the intelligent carnivores again, particularly at night.

"I think so," SStragh said.

Jennifer looked up and down the trail. Off to the left was a thick cluster of giant ferns. She gestured towards the grove. "We'd better hide."

"I do not need to hide from *Gairk*," SStragh said mulishly, even though she looked almost ready to fall asleep.

SStragh regarded her silently for a long heartbeat. The thrashing in the brush came ever closer. Even though Jennifer was beginning to understand how SStragh's mind worked, there was still no telling how the Mutata would react in a given situation. Even though SStragh had human-level intelligence, her culture viewed the world and concepts like life and death differently than humans did. SStragh did crazy things sometimes—at least they seemed crazy to Jennifer, but they were perfectly sensible to the Mutata.

The sounds were very close now.

"I will hide if you think we must," SStragh finally said, and headed toward the fern grove.

Jennifer breathed a sigh of relief and followed. They had barely settled into cover, out of sight and downwind from the trail, when two heavily armed Gairk burst into view. Jennifer recognized the lead dinosaur as he rushed by in the dappled moonlight. It was Klaido, the Gairk whose life Jennifer had saved, the Gairk who had vowed to kill Peter and Eckels. He and his companion took the left-hand fork, passing Jennifer and SStragh's hiding place without giving it a second glance.

"Did you see him, SStragh?"

"Yes. It was Klaido," SStragh said. "To see Gairk about at night means one thing. They are hunting and have caught the scent. Not even the dark can call them off their prey."

"Peter . . ." Jennifer whispered, suddenly feeling as if a cold breeze had blown across the back of her neck. Jennifer swallowed hard. "Maybe we'd better follow them."

If the Gairk were on his trail, Peter needed their help. What little they could give.

3

Out of the Frying Pan

Eckels went to the back of the cave. Peter followed and watched as he stopped before a sheet of flagstone tipped up against the wall. The stone was a rough rectangle about four feet tall and three wide, but only a few inches thick. It rested on one of its short sides. Eckels gestured at it with his torch.

"Push that aside, will you?"

Peter looked at him. "Why?"

Eckels sighed. "Because it's blocking our way. Come on, we haven't got all night."

Peter cupped his fingers around the edge of the stone and heaved. The piece was heavy, but once he got it moving gravity did the rest. The slab slid gratingly down the wall and smacked the floor with a hollow boom, exposing a hole about a foot and a half in diameter in the cave wall. It was much too smooth to be entirely natural.

"You must have been here a good while before you were captured," Peter commented. "Took a lot of work to carve the rock like that."

Eckels shrugged, though he looked irritated. "I guess. Like I said before, I don't remember any of it—I don't remember this cave, I don't remember capturing you and the girl, and I don't remember most of the killing the lizards say I did. I must've been out of my head a long time after the explosion." Eckels gave a quick shiver, then hunkered down before the hole, looking in. "This passage ends about ten feet in."

"Ten feet?" Peter asked. "What good is a lousy ten feet? We can't hole up in there. The Gairk'll just starve us out."

"Have some faith, Peter," Eckels said with one of his indulgent smiles. "Whether I can recall choosing this cave or not, I must have done so quite deliberately. Intelligently. You should never have a stronghold without a back door. And this," he said gesturing dramatically with his torch, "is our back door."

Peter eyed the tunnel dubiously.

"Follow me, kid," Eckels said. "Or stay behind and become a snack for the Gairk. I don't care." Eckels smiled, lay down, and wormed his way into the hole headfirst. Peter watched him kick and wiggle until his feet disappeared.

"Eckels?" Peter called.

There was no reply. Peter took a deep breath. He hated closed, confined spaces. This little adventure seemed destined to play to all his worst fears. He looked anxiously around the cave. He couldn't possibly force himself into that tiny little hole leading into the center of the hill. What if the tunnel got even narrower, becoming smaller and smaller until he became stuck while his torch burned down to nothing and left him in utter blackness with the rock pressing in all around . . .

Peter tried to push away that line of thought, but it was difficult. Eckels was a small man. He might be able to worm his way through the passage. But Peter was bigger than Eckels, with broader shoulders and a deeper chest. If the tunnel narrowed and he got stuck, he'd stay there until he died of thirst or hunger, entombed like a coffinless mummy in the heart of the hill. He couldn't possibly follow Eckels.

A loud crash echoed thunderously from the cave mouth. The Gairk, Peter realized, were tired of waiting for their prey to come out. They were ripping aside boulders to get into the cave entrance. Peter realized that he couldn't stay here much longer. What choice did he have?

He threw himself on the floor and peered into the cramped tunnel. By the flickering light of his companion's torch, Peter could see that Eckels had made it to the end of the passageway. All he could see were Eckels's legs from the knees down. Eckels seemed to be standing in an opening about ten feet down the tunnel. As Peter watched, Eckels's legs disappeared as he began to climb.

Peter suddenly understood. This passageway led to a vent, a vertical chimney leading upward, presumably opening onto the hill's surface.

Knowing that escape wasn't just a figment of Eckels's imagination galvanized Peter. Blanking all conscious thought from his mind, Peter lighted his own torch, flipped onto his back, and squirmed through the opening just as Eckels had.

The tunnel *was* a much tighter fit for Peter. His shoulders scraped both walls and the solid rock ceiling was no more than half a foot from the tip of his nose. But somehow he managed to inch along with his legs and one arm, pushing the torch ahead with his other arm.

Thank God for the light, Peter thought. If he'd had to crawl into darkness, he knew he couldn't make it.

It was still hard going. The struggle to wriggle ten feet to the end of the passageway seemed to take forever. Finally the torch hit solid rock, sprayed a shower of sparks, and nearly went out. Looking upward, Peter could see a vague patch of starry night sky intermittently eclipsed by Eckels's body. Eckels was working his way up the vent like Santa going up a chimney. Peter couldn't judge how high Eckels had gone, but it had to be at least twenty feet.

"Eckels!" Peter shouted, but the man made no reply.

Okay, Peter thought. *If he can do it, so can I.*

The vent's opening was actually fairly wide, almost four feet across. Peter extended his arms up into the crevice, then inched his way back, slowly standing and squirming around Eckels's abandoned torch, snuffed out on the tunnel floor but still hot to the touch. It was hard on his legs, but Peter was strong and in good condition from his football training. In a minute or so he was standing upright in the narrow vent, breathing heavily and resting against the solid rock as the sweat that had gathered on his forehead dripped down into his eyes and off his nose.

Peter tilted his head back and looked up the crack to see a clear and unobstructed view of the night sky. The stars seemed awfully far away.

"Eckels!" Peter shouted again. "Hey, Eckels! I'm coming up! Wait for me!"

He stared up anxiously. After a moment something blotted out part of the opening and a pale oval face peered down at him. Then the face vanished.

Peter took a deep breath. "I'm coming," he said in a quiet voice.

He braced his back against the wall and put his right foot six inches up against the opposite wall. He quickly brought his left foot up next to his right and hung for a moment, braced solidly against opposing walls.

Peter had seen rock climbers scale chimneys like these on television, though he'd never tried it himself. He knew what he had to do. He had to work his way upward inch by inch, keeping himself wedged in the space between the walls. It hadn't looked particularly difficult on television, but this was for real.

Peter realized that he had to drop the torch. Holding it over his head was straining his right arm to the point of numbness, and he needed both hands to help him up the rough stone surface. Eckels had dropped his torch before attempting the ascent—Peter could see the snuffed-out brand on the tunnel floor below.

Fortunately, the vent was wider than the cramped tunnel which led to it. Peter extended his arm and let the torch drop. The branch hit the floor a foot below him, burning with a dim, guttering light.

Peter hated to lose the torch, but he didn't waste time worrying about it. Pushing hard with his legs, arms, back, and shoulders, he started to inch his way up the wall. It was easier when he used both hands. The rough unevenness of the stone helped his grip, but was hard on his flesh. Fighting gravity and his own fear, he was soon soaked with sweat despite the coolness of the surrounding rock. For a moment he had the horrible thought that if the rock shifted, if the layer upon layer of sediment that made up the hill slipped just the tiniest bit, the fissure would close and squash him to jelly.

He would have cried or maybe laughed, but he didn't have the breath for it. He was laboring hard. By the time he'd made only a few feet of the climb his T-shirt was in tatters. He could feel the rough stone surface tear his flesh and he wondered if the substance soaking his torn shirt was sweat or blood.

Eckels made it, he told himself. *Eckels made it and I will too.*

Peter hauled himself up another foot. His legs were shaking with fatigue. His hands were numb from the constant pressure and contact with the cold stone. His back was a mass of cuts and the sweat burned as it ran into his open wounds.

Peter knew he needed to rest and catch his breath. Just a moment, then he'd go on. He stopped, but when his breathing had slowed and he tried to push ahead he couldn't. He just couldn't. It was as if all his strength had left him. He felt helpless as panic ran cold through his brain. All he could do was cling to the rock walls and shiver.

One inch, he told himself. *That's all.* He forced his right foot up, then his left. *There, that's not so hard . . .*

Peter pushed with both arms against the opposite wall and wiggled like a snake, gaining another two inches. He slung his right leg up once more, then his left, but suddenly his tired muscles cramped. Pain shot through his left leg as if a knife had been stuck in his calf. Muscles knotted and his grip loosened. His left foot slipped free, then his right started to go and he knew he was falling.

Peter screamed.

From nowhere a hand reached out and grabbed his right arm. It heaved with extraordinary strength, pulling him up so another hand could grasp his left arm. The hands were dark and hairy with coarse, clumsy fingers that had strange webbing between them. They looked like an ape's hands, and were just as strong. Peter didn't have any time to think about it. He popped out of the vent's opening like a cork out of a bottle, and was pulled to the safety of solid ground.

"Eckels?" Peter muttered.

He looked around, but Eckels was nowhere in sight. The first person he focused on was Travis, the man from the future who had stumbled into Peter's timeline while hunting Eckels. Next to him an apelike creature with an almost comically serious expression on its leathery, wrinkled face. And the third person—

"Aaron! " Peter exclaimed.

His friend hovered over him with anxiety and concern.

"Peter, where's Jennifer? Have you seen Grandpa Carl?"

"Jennifer!" Peter burst out. "What about me? We both went looking for you, after all—"

"You mentioned Eckels a moment ago," Travis interrupted. "Is he with you?"

"Sure—" Peter began.

"Damn!" Travis interrupted. He turned to Aaron. "I told you it was Eckels. I'd recognize that rat anywhere! You should've let me go after him—"

"If we'd gone off chasing Eckels," Aaron said with quiet authority, "Peter would have fallen and died. I told you I heard someone calling for help."

"Yeah, you're right," Travis said gruffly. "But we got the kid now. Let's get after that no good—"

"Isn't anyone," Mundo interrupted with pompous gravity, "going to introduce me?"

Clouds scudded across the moon like wrecked ships floating on a black sea.

"I don't like the way the air smells," SStragh said.

Jennifer nodded. Her sense of smell wasn't as sharp as her companion's, but even she could taste a strangeness in the air—strangeness she had felt before.

"A Dreaming Storm is brewing," she said quietly.

Such storms ripped through the Mutata valley with increasing ferocity and frequency, causing tremendous destruction with their swirling winds and startling lightning displays. Pockets of temporal instability appeared everywhere in the storms' paths. Pieces of alternate realities, some as familiar as yesterday, others more alien than anything Jennifer could imagine, popped into brief existence and then vanished with the storms' passings.

"I'm sure these storms are connected with the Floating Paths and the openings into time," Jennifer said. "I wonder if one of the paths is nearby."

SStragh made an odd sound, like a steam kettle overheating. She looked away from Jennifer.

"There *is* one near, isn't there?"

Another hiss escaped from her reptilian friend. "Yes," SStragh said finally. "After Peeitah and Eikels left the village, the OColi insisted that the Floating Stones be moved so the humans couldn't use them to leave our world. The Floating Stone from which the hard-shelled humans come is very near here." She pointed with her spear. "That way."

The hard-shelled humans—she meant the samurai, Jennifer realized. "Where's the Stone that leads to my world?" Jennifer asked. "The one that leads back to Green Town?"

SStragh lifted her head. "The OColi has said that I may not tell you."

There was no arguing with a direct order from the OColi. Jennifer knew that SStragh would obey such a directive no matter how she personally felt. "Then let's go see this other one. This could be important. Peter and Eckels will keep for now. Besides, it's opposite the direction the Gairk took. I'm not sure that I want to deal with an armed party of those guys."

"You may be wise," SStragh said solemnly. "All right. First we shall go see this Floating Stone. *Then* we shall find Peeitah and Eikels. Right?"

Jennifer nodded. SStragh was learning enough about human body language to make sense of its simpler expressions.

"Lead the way," Jennifer told her companion.

The sense of wrongness in the air seemed to increase as they neared the piece of roadway that had been blasted into the Mutata timeline. Not only were the bits of roadway frightening artifacts of an alien technology that threatened the fabric of the OColihi, but this particular one was also the source of the samurai warriors whom Jennifer had seen when she had first entered the dinosaur world.

The samurai had come through frequently when the roadway had first appeared in the Mutata valley. They'd arrived in twos and threes, seemingly intent on scouting the area and also seeking combat with the Mutata and Gairk. When the Mutata had discovered that the Floating Stone was the source of these invasions, they'd mounted a guard over it. The attacks had slowed to a trickle. Some samurai occasionally still came through, but rarely could they elude the Mutata spears awaiting them.

SStragh suddenly stopped. She lowered her voice to a quiet rumble. "The Floating Stone is there, beyond that grove. If we get much closer, the sentries will see us. The OColi did not say I couldn't bring you here, but . . ."

"But he would also be upset if he knew," Jennifer finished. "Fine. I agree. Is there a place we can watch the Floating Stone and not be seen?"

"This way," SStragh said.

The stone lay in a bowl-shaped clearing in the forest, sheltered by a thick stand of trees. Opposite the trees, across the clearing, a convenient rock outcrop offered more than adequate cover.

As SStragh and Jennifer made their way to the outcropping they saw the roadway and the Mutata sentries guarding it illuminated by a roaring fire. Two Mutata kept vigil near the alien artifact, using the fire to ward off the chill night.

"How long do we wait?" SStragh asked Jennifer as quietly as she could as they settled down among the rocks.

"It's still early. We can stay here an hour or so and still have time to find Peter and Eckels."

SStragh looked wistfully toward the fire. "I hope," she said, "the wait won't be too long."

4

Into the Fire

"Of course it's great to see you, Peter," Aaron said. "And this is Mundo. He's . . ." Aaron was momentarily at a loss to explain. ". . . not from here."

"I can see that," Peter said, his joy at finding other humans tempered by his anger at Eckels's desertion.

Aaron looked critically at his onetime closest friend. "You look like you've been put through a wringer."

"I have," Peter said. "First me and Jennifer were captured by those intelligent lizards, then we escaped and I've been stuck living in a cave for weeks with Eckels—"

Aaron and Travis interrupted simultaneously.

"Jennifer—how is she?"

"Eckels—he's getting away!"

"Jennifer's fine," Peter said tiredly. "She made friends with one of the lizards and even learned its language. It's just a bunch of honking and snorting to me." He shook his head. "And Eckels . . . there's nowhere he can go."

"Wait a minute," Aaron said suddenly, "you said you and Eckels have been with each other for weeks, and all three of you were together a long time before that. You're

37

talking *months*. But we've been separated for only two weeks, tops . . ."

Aaron's voice trailed off as he realized that the situation was even more complicated than that. It had been twelve *years* for Grandpa Carl. Twelve years in Green Town, a few months for Peter, two weeks for him and Travis . . .

"I know the difference between months and weeks," Peter said. "Believe me, I know exactly how long I've been stuck in this place."

"Okay," Aaron said. "Things are all tangled up. It seems that time must run at different speeds on different parts of the path."

"Meanwhile," Peter said, "while we're sitting here jawing, the Gairks could be sneaking up on us."

"Gairks?" Aaron said. "What are those?"

A sudden bone-chilling roar froze them all. Aaron and Travis both turned to stare at the bipedal reptile coming toward them, roaring a challenge and waving a huge war club threateningly. Peter smiled with some satisfaction at the stupefied expression on their faces.

"That," he said, "is a Gairk."

His satisfaction was short-lived. The Gairk lumbered toward them with the speed of an express train.

"Talk to it," Aaron said. "Tell it we're friends."

"I can't," Peter said in a clipped, strained voice. "Shoot it."

"Shoot it! Shoot it!" Mundo urged, jumping up and down in agitation.

Travis didn't need encouragement. He snapped his rifle up to his shoulder, aimed, and squeezed off a shot. The report was deafening in the still night.

The bullet struck the Gairk high on the chest. It punched through the armor as if it were tinfoil and penetrated deeply into meat and muscle. But the Gairk still came on.

"Aim for its head," Peter urged, backing up. Mundo had already turned and fled, heading for the single tree that grew on the hilltop.

The Gairk was almost upon them. Aaron watched it, dazed. It was the strangest thing he'd seen so far on his cross-time quest. It was definitely an allosaur, though smaller than the terrors that had haunted the past of his own time. But intelligent, obviously. He—if the reptile was a he—wore armor and trinkets and carried a weapon. Evolution had taken a very weird turn in this timeline.

Aaron wanted to talk to him and discover the alien sensibilities a reptilian intelligence would evolve. But he could see that the Gairk was in no mood to discuss philosophy. He was coming to kill.

Travis squeezed off a second shot, shouting, "Scatter."

It was good advice. The Gairk would be among them in seconds. Even if Travis's aim was true, there was no guarantee that a single bullet would stop it. Aaron jumped to the side, tripped, and fell, then realized with horror that the Gairk had fixated on him. The dinosaur loomed over him. Roaring in triumph, it lifted its club to strike.

Aaron scuttled backward as the reptile slowly tilted forward and with the ponderous dignity of a falling redwood tree crashed to the ground right at Aaron's feet. Aaron took a deep breath, trying to slow his racing heart. It was a moment before he felt calm enough to speak.

"Too bad you had to shoot him," he said in a voice that was almost steady. "I would've liked to talk with him."

"There's plenty more where he came from," Peter said. "You'll get your chance if we don't get out of here."

"The boy's right," Travis said. "Let's go."

Aaron climbed to his feet. "All right. Where?"

"After Eckels." Travis's voice was grim. He held his rifle like he still wanted to use it. "I think he went in that direction."

"Okay. That's as good a direction as any," Aaron said. All he had to do now, he thought, was figure out a way to keep Travis from shooting Eckels on sight. Well, he'd deal with that problem when the time came. They might not even be able to find Eckels, at least not right away. There were plenty of places to hide in the forest.

"What's that noise?" Peter asked.

"What?"

"That kind of wailing."

Aaron and Travis exchanged horrified glances.

"He found the time machine!" Travis said behind clenched teeth.

"You have a time machine?" Peter asked. "You can get us out of here? What if Eckels takes off and maroons us?"

"He can't," Aaron said. "I disabled the temporal controls just before we left the ship." He turned to the tree where Mundo was hiding and waved. "Come on," he shouted. "Let's go."

Mundo dropped down to the ground with practiced agility and strolled over to join them with an equally practiced nonchalance. "What are we doing?" he asked.

"We have to recover the time machine," Aaron replied. "And then," he said, voicing the need that had been in the front of his mind ever since Peter had mentioned her name, "we're going to find Jennifer."

"What's that sound?" Jennifer asked.

It was a noise neither she, nor certainly SStragh, had ever heard before. It was a wailing ululating whine similar to that of a police siren with a grating, high-pitched whirring component that was totally unfamiliar to Jennifer's ears.

SStragh gave the equivalent of a Mutata frown by flexing her lips back and showing her teeth, but before she could say anything, chaos erupted around them.

A strange vehicle—*Vehicle*, Jennifer thought, *on the dinosaur world?*—broke into the clearing in front of the Floating Stone. SStragh drew back, her spinal crest raised in astonished fear. The vehicle, source of the piercing wail, was unlike anything Jennifer had ever seen. It was armored like a light tank, but had no treads or weapons protruding from it. It had a clear windshield in the front. As it rumbled past, Jennifer thought she saw Eckels at the controls, then she dismissed that possibility from her mind. It couldn't be Eckels. If he had this machine, why would he live in a cave?

It didn't move very fast, especially since the driver had to weave around trees and moderate-size stones, but it moved quickly enough to be upon the Mutata guards before they knew what was happening.

One of the guards stood directly in its path. Despite the fear disclosed by the Mutata's body language, she refused to back down. The sentry flung her spear at the inexorably approaching vehicle. The weapon clattered off harmlessly and by then it was too late for the Mutata to move.

She screamed thinly as the vehicle smashed into her. Her screams choked off into a hideous gurgle as the machine rolled serenely over her and headed right for the Floating Stone.

The other sentry charged it from the side. His spear splintered against the vehicle and he was knocked to the ground by the force of the impact.

SStragh screamed a challenge and leapt out of concealment, running as quickly as she could toward the battle. Jennifer jumped after her, yelling, "Wait! SStragh, wait!"

But it was too late.

The vehicle touched the Floating Stone and the time storm, threatening all evening, broke with the force of a sudden hurricane. Lightning exploded in the sky. Clouds burst, whipping up a sudden wailing wind that almost knocked Jennifer off her feet. The dirt thrown up by the gusts made it difficult to see as the flashes of lightning illuminated bizarre scenes like snippets of movies made in some other time and place.

The first scene was that of a Japanese building with a slanting tile roof. The vehicle vanished as the building quickly faded and other vistas took its place.

A steep-sided stone pyramid appeared. A line of people was snaking up its side. The people, men and women both, looked tired and afraid. Jennifer could almost see what was going on at the top of the pyramid, then it vanished in a flash of lightning to be replaced with a Roman-style marble temple.

A man in a plumed helmet and bronze breastplate stared at Jennifer. He shouted words to her that sounded like Latin, but the wind was moaning so loudly she couldn't quite make them out. His face was a mask of terror, but he too vanished in moments.

There were no buildings in the next scene, only endless, sunny cliffs overlooking a tumultuous ocean. Great pterodactyls flew in the bright blue sky. Jennifer immediately recognized them as saorods, intelligent winged dinosaurs who had assaulted the Mutata village some days ago. One flashed by, caught on the tempestuous wind currents—flashed by, Jennifer realized, out of its own world and into theirs.

Its world vanished as the time storm passed out. The saorod screeched in fear and anger and banked suddenly, turned on Jennifer. Like the Gairk, their initial response to any threat was violence, and this saorod felt very, very threatened.

It screamed as it swooped down upon Jennifer, its talons extended, its jaws opened wide. Jennifer had no weapon to fend it off and no time to dodge. She fell to the earth, instinctively curled up into a ball, protecting her head and stomach, expecting at any second to feel the saorod's razor-sharp talons tear into her flesh.

Above her came the sound of thunder.

The saorod squawked and plummeted to the earth, crashing right beside Jennifer. She took her arms from around her head and looked right into its eyes. It almost seemed as if she could read pain and surprise there, then the saorod shuddered all over and its eyes closed.

"Jennifer!"

She couldn't believe her ears. She looked up, stunned and deliriously happy at the same time.

"Aaron!"

He reached her side as she leapt to her feet. They hugged fiercely. "It's been so long," she said, trying not to cry as her face nestled into the side of Aaron's neck and shoulder.

"It's been two weeks for me," he said, "but even that was too long."

Finally they broke the embrace and held each other at arm's length.

"Let me look at you," they both started to say, stopped, and laughed.

"Well, isn't this a cozy reunion," Peter said. He tried to make it sound lighthearted, but there was a bite to the words that both Aaron and Jennifer noticed.

Jennifer looked at him and nodded. Behind him stood Travis, his gun barrel resting casually over his shoulder.

"Thanks," Jennifer told the guide. "The saorod would have got me for sure."

"Is that what you call them?" Aaron asked, hunkered down over the corpse.

"That's what the Mutata call them."

"So you really speak their language? That's great. I'd like to meet one of these intelligent dinosaurs."

Jennifer nodded. "That's no problem. SStragh—" She stopped, looking around. SStragh was gone. Jennifer stopped to think. The last time she'd seen SStragh, the Mutata had been chasing the strange vehicle . . . right onto the Floating Stone.

"Oh, no," Jennifer said.

"What?" Aaron looked up from the saorod corpse.

"My friend, SStragh. She followed that machine, whatever it was, up onto the Floating Stone. She's gone."

Travis was tight-lipped. "He's gone, too."

"He?" Jennifer asked. "Not Eckels?"

"Eckels," Travis said. "He stole our time machine."

Peter sank down to the ground with an audible sigh. "Great. There goes our ticket home."

"Time machine?" Jennifer asked. "Could it really have taken us home?"

He decided that it wasn't the time to get into a complicated explanation. That could wait for later, when everything had calmed down. "Maybe," he said. "It sure was our best chance, anyway."

"Well what are we waiting for?" Travis asked. "Let's go get him."

"Do you have any idea where this roadway leads?" Aaron asked.

"To some kind of oriental world. Probably Japanese."

"Japanese, huh?" Peter said. "That's got to be better than two-legged talking lizards."

"Like I said," Travis said in an edgy voice, "what are we waiting for?"

Aaron nodded. They had to go after Eckels, no matter how strange or dangerous this new world. The time machine was still their best chance of finding their way back to their home timeline, as slim as that hope was.

"We're waiting," Aaron said, "for Mundo to come out from behind those trees. It's safe now," he called. "I want you to meet my friend Jennifer."

Mundo poked his head out from behind a tree. "Pleased to meet you, Jennifer."

Jennifer stared at him. "Pleased to meet you, too."

"No more talk," Travis said. "It's time we got after Eckels."

He slung his rifle over his shoulder and stepped toward the roadway.

5

The Land of the Rising Sun

"We can't go in unprepared," Aaron said, remembering the difficulties he'd had when he'd plunged into the changed Green Town. "We don't know what'll be waiting for us on the other side."

"Eckels," Travis said. "That's enough for me."

"And SStragh," Jennifer added. "She may be in trouble."

"Still worried about your lizard friends," Peter muttered.

"That's right," Jennifer shot back. "People worry about their friends, Peter. Maybe that's a concept you're not familiar with."

Peter's face reddened.

"Arguing won't solve anything," Aaron said. "We've got to stick together and watch out for each other. No one else will. It's just the four of us—"

"And me," Mundo chipped in.

"All right, the five of us against an entire world. We can't waste our energy bickering among ourselves. Right?"

47

"Right," Jennifer admitted.

Peter gave a sullen nod.

"Okay," Aaron said. "Is there anything we can take along to make the trip safer?"

"All our weapons and supplies were in the time machine," Travis pointed out. "Now Eckels has them all."

"Right," Aaron said. "Peter, how about that cave of yours? Anything worth bringing along?"

"If you want to risk meeting up with a bunch of Gairk for a couple of clay pots, be my guest," he said ungraciously.

"Riiight," Aaron said in a slow voice. It seemed that Peter's time in the dinosaur world had made him even more caustic. But they had to worry about survival first and soothing Peter's ego second. Aaron turned to Jennifer. "How about the Muta?" he asked. "Can we get any help from them?"

"Mutata," Jennifer corrected automatically, putting a reasonably close facsimile of the proper roar between the syllables. She shook her head. "No. SStragh was among a minority of Mutata who were willing to listen to me. I'm afraid that if we went back to their village and told them what happened, the odds of us getting out again wouldn't be too good."

Aaron nodded. "I guess it is us against the world." He looked at Travis. "Any time you're ready."

Travis nodded grimly. "I'm ready now," he said. His face was gaunt, showing the pain of his recent physical wounds and mental trauma.

He stepped onto the bit of temporal roadway floating inches off the ground and immediately disappeared.

"Quick," Aaron said, "after him."

They followed at an interval of two or three seconds apiece. Jennifer went first, after a warm glance back at

Aaron. Instinctively he seemed to know what she was thinking. They'd just found one another and she didn't want them to be separated again. Well, with any luck they wouldn't be. It was possible that Green Town might be lost forever, Aaron thought, but as long as he had Jennifer it didn't seem quite so bad.

Of course, his grandfather was still lost somewhere on this world. But splitting their slim forces wouldn't be wise even if he knew where to look for Grandpa Carl. He just had to pray that his grandfather could take care of himself until they all returned with the time machine.

Peter went next, also after a glance back at Aaron, his expression more enigmatic than Jennifer's. It was a mixture of worry and fear, with maybe a hint that he was glad to be with Aaron again. Maybe. Well, they'd been best friends once. Maybe this adventure would heal the rift, or forever tear them apart.

Mundo followed Peter. He was the unpredictable variable, the wild card of the group. Aaron was sorry they'd ever met and even sorrier that he'd talked Mundo into accompanying them. But now that the creature was with them, Aaron was responsible for him. He was responsible for them all.

He waited until Mundo had disappeared, then took a deep breath and stepped upon the bit of temporal roadway. He wondered where it would take him.

Cold bit at him with razor-edged teeth. Nausea whirled him head over heels until he thought he would throw up. Then the transition was complete and Aaron caught himself taking a step forward, the way you do when there's one less riser than expected at the bottom of a stairway. He almost stumbled, then oriented himself, blinking.

He'd gone from night to day, from coolness to pleasant warmth, from outdoors to indoors.

He was alone inside a small, simple, single-room structure, apparently a shrine of some sort. The floor and walls
were wooden planks. A couple of plain wood pillars
helped hold up the roof. A huge altar dominated the far
end of the room. Small tablets set in wooden bases stood
like tiny headstones on the altar amid a number of burning candles. The tablets were inscribed with oriental-
looking writing—Japanese, probably. A piece of temporal
roadway floated several inches above the floor in front of
the altar.

A hole big enough to drive a time machine through
had been punched through one of the shrine's walls. And
there was a body lying face down in front of the altar,
drenched in a pool of blood.

"Oh, no," Aaron whispered. He stuck his head through
the hole in the wall. "Where is everybody?" he called out.

"Here," Jennifer answered from somewhere in front of
the temple.

Aaron gingerly climbed down to the ground and
picked his way through the pile of shattered wood-scrap
that had once been most of a wall. He looked around.

Around him was a forest. It was a real forest with
familiar trees, grasses, and shrubs, not some kind of pale-
ontologist's jumbled dream. For a moment Aaron
thought they might have found their home reality, but
realized, of course, there were no Japanese shrines in the
forests of his Illinois.

The building definitely looked Japanese. Aaron studied
it closely as he rounded the corner. He'd seen pictures of
similar structures in books about Japan. No doubt about it.

Then he saw more bodies.

There were three of them. They had met recent, vio-
lent deaths. Jennifer was kneeling before one, trying to

find a pulse. She looked up just as Aaron focused on her, turned, and caught his eye. She let the corpse's wrist drop and shook her head.

"What happened to them?" Aaron asked.

"Eckels," Travis spit. "This is more of his work."

Aaron looked closely at the bodies, details registering for the first time. They'd been short, stocky men, wearing clothing from an earlier century. Only one had a weapon, a sword clutched in his hand. The others were unarmed. All three had been shot numerous times, presumably by an automatic weapon from the time machine.

"He went that way," Travis said. He was hunkered down by the traces left by the time machine, pointing off into the forest.

"Are there any signs of SStragh?" Jennifer asked.

Travis followed the track of the time machine for a few feet, his head down, his eyes intent and searching.

"Here's a track," he said after a moment. "It's got to be her, unless there're other reptiles walking on two legs in this world."

"She's following Eckels," Jennifer said. "We have to go after her."

"That might not be a good idea," Mundo said. "We don't know what's out there in the forest."

"That's why we can't desert SStragh," Jennifer said, a touch of anger in her voice.

"I agree with Mundo," Peter said.

"Running off without thinking—" Mundo began, but Aaron stopped him with a shout.

"Look!" He pointed into the woods. "Something's moving behind those trees!

"I see it!" yelled Travis. He aimed his rifle.

"Wait!" Jennifer called. "Don't shoot!"

She shouted a few words in Japanese, hoping that her high school vocabulary and diction would be good enough to communicate in this world. Evidently they were, for after a moment's hesitation a face peered uncertainly around the trunk of a great oak tree. Jennifer held her hands up, showing that she had no weapons, and started to walk toward the stand of trees.

"Jennifer," Aaron called, "be careful!"

"I will," she answered calmly. "It's all right."

She switched to Japanese again, talking in a soothing voice. She stopped about halfway to the tree and fell silent, beckoning for whoever was hiding to come out into the open.

It was a boy, younger than any of the marooned time travelers. Bewildered and frightened-looking, he was dressed in the simple clothing of a peasant. He was unarmed.

"Don't worry," Jennifer told him in Japanese. "We won't hurt you. What's your name?"

He was silent for a moment, but then said, "Katsu."

"I am Jennifer." She gestured behind herself at the others. "These are my friends. We won't hurt you."

Katsu looked them over quickly and nodded nervously. "Is that a monkey?" he asked, pointing at Mundo. "I have heard tales of monkeys."

"Monkey?" Mundo bristled, understanding perfectly and replying in much better Japanese than that spoken by Jennifer. "I am not a monkey. I am Mundo."

Aaron didn't know who was more startled by Mundo's sudden fluency in Japanese, himself or the boy, Katsu. Then Aaron realized that he shouldn't be surprised. Mundo, after all, could skim surface thoughts and understand new languages almost instantaneously. He'd picked up English in the same way.

For a second it looked as if Katsu was going to try to run in three different directions at once, but he settled down and stared at Mundo in awe.

"This is truly a day for wonders," he said. "Are you the Monkey King?"

Jennifer looked at Mundo warily. The Monkey King was a supernatural being of Japanese legend. He had the reputation of being a clown, but was also a sly trickster who frequently helped common people in need. It wouldn't hurt to have someone in their party identified with the legendary creature.

"Monkey King?" Mundo repeated. "Why, yes, of course that's who I am. And they," he waved grandly at Jennifer and the others, "are my comrades."

"Do you come from the Land Beyond the Stone?" Katsu asked in a soft voice.

"That's right," Jennifer said, taking over from Mundo. "We've come searching for something that was stolen from us. Did you see what happened here, Katsu?"

The boy nodded. "I was sweeping the Shrine of the Floating Stone," he said. "That's one of my jobs. The Floating Stone leads to the Land of the Dragons. Samurai go there to prove their bravery and earn the red sash. Common people like me used to be able to go there also and those who returned would be raised to the rank of samurai. But Lord Akira put an end to that when he came to our village last year. He said we were losing too many men." Katsu looked downcast. "So now I will never earn a second name and the right to carry two swords.

As Katsu spoke Jennifer translated as best she could. He seemed to be speaking an archaic form of Japanese, but Jennifer could understand most of what he said.

He stopped for a moment and Jennifer prompted him to go on with his story.

"I was sweeping the floor," Katsu continued, "when suddenly a great . . . a great thing came from beyond the Stone. It was like a turtle, with a man inside, guiding it. I have never seen its like before."

"What happened then?" Jennifer asked.

"It . . . it ran right over Harada—one of the priests— and I got frightened and hid behind the altar. Then, outside, I heard great noises, like someone was firing arquebuses, but much faster than any man could fire. There were screams, then silence. When I looked out the hole the turtle had made in the wall, I saw the other two priests and the samurai on guard duty lying on the ground. I went out and looked closely, but they were dead. I heard something else moving in the shrine. I hid."

"Did you see who else was in the shrine?"

Katsu shook his head. "I was frightened. I hid in the trees and didn't look."

It must have been SStragh, Jennifer thought. It was just as well Katsu didn't see her. He'd had enough shocks for one day.

Mundo pointed. "Look there," he said in English.

A trail wound through the forest. Several hundred yards distant a troop of angry-looking samurai was coming toward them. Their leader was on horseback; the others were on foot.

"We'd better run," Peter said. "We can lose them in the woods."

"They probably know the woods a lot better than we do," Aaron said. "They'd round us up in minutes."

"Then we'd better arm ourselves," Peter said. He stooped down and took the sword from the dead samurai's hand.

"No!" Aaron said. "Our only chance is to make friends with them."

"Who elected you leader?" Peter asked angrily. "What if they don't want to make friends?"

"Aaron's right," Jennifer said quietly. "We can't kill everyone on this whole world. That's something Eckels would do. We have to find allies if we want to accomplish anything."

"What do you say, Travis?" Peter said, turning to the older man.

Travis sighed deeply. "I say Aaron and Jennifer are right."

Peter turned to Mundo, but the ape only shrugged, then positioned himself close to a nearby tree. Peter threw the sword angrily to the ground.

"You're nuts. They'll kill us all."

"I don't think so," Aaron said.

"Katsu," Jennifer said, "do you know who leads the samurai?"

Katsu bobbed his head. "That is Captain Otomo. He leads all samurai for Lord Akira."

Jennifer nodded.

They waited quietly, Travis with his rifle dangling casually from its carrying strap. He and Aaron exchanged nods. Aaron knew that the hunter would be ready to give them a fighting chance if Otomo chose to attack without talking.

They could make out more details as the samurai got closer. The man on horseback was armored in traditional samurai fashion. An intricate work of art as well as as a practical means of defense, his armor consisted of a body piece of thousands of metal scales riveted together into a seamless whole. Separate pieces protected his arms from shoulder to fingertips and a matching helmet perched atop his head. Sunlight shone off the burnished armor like the scales of a rainbow trout flashing brightly in a shallow stream. He carried a long spear and had two swords, a long and a short one, sheathed at his waist. The footmen streaming out behind him had various weapons. Most had spears, but half a dozen of them carried bows. Another three had what looked like primitive muskets of some kind. The foot soldiers were all bare-legged, but had body armor that was neither as intricate nor as colorful as that worn by Otomo. All the foot soldiers also had little flags fluttering behind them on short poles set in sockets in the back plates of their body armor. The design was a simple, familiar one. It was a red circle on a pure white background, the symbol of the rising sun.

"How'd we end up in Japan?" Peter asked.

"I don't think we *are* in Japan," Jennifer replied. "Look in the forest close to the edge of the trail."

Half a dozen men were coming toward them through the forest. They were dressed in loincloths and leather leggings. Their hair was long and black, with feathers stuck in it for ornamentation. It was difficult to discern many details because they were moving quickly through cover and dappled sunlight, but there was no doubt that they were American Indians.

"What's going on here?" Aaron asked quietly.

"We'll find out soon," Travis said dryly as the mounted samurai reined in before them.

He was a young man, stern and harsh-looking, but it was difficult to read his expression because of the metal mask that covered the lower half of his face. His flashing eyes took in the newcomers, glanced at the bodies, then Katsu. He shouted a single harsh word of command and the foot soldiers fanned out, effectively surrounding Aaron and the others. The archers stood ready, as did the men armed with the primitive firearms. The Indians, too, had come out from the cover of the forest and stood dispersed among the samurai.

No one looked happy to see the newcomers.

"These guys look like they mean business," Peter said. "I told you we should have tried to get away."

Aaron tried to put a smile on his face and nodded reassuringly at the mounted samurai as he answered Peter. "You see those Indian scouts? How far do you think we would have got?"

Peter shook his head but didn't say anything as Otomo barked out another command. One of the Indians stepped forward and spoke expectantly in a flowing, multisyllabic language.

"Sorry," Aaron said. He tried to keep his friendly smile as he shook his head. "But we don't understand. We're not from around here."

"But," Jennifer said to Otomo in Japanese, "I can understand you."

The Indian frowned. He glanced back at the samurai, who barked out another command. The Indian rejoined the circle of soldiers as Otomo suddenly dismounted.

One of the foot soldiers broke from the circle and grabbed the reins as Otomo threw them back over his shoulder without looking. Otomo handed his spear to another foot soldier, then strode forward boldly, his hand on the hilt of his sheathed long sword.

"You speak our language?"

Even those who didn't understand his words could detect the disbelief in his voice.

"I do," Jennifer said.

The officer stared at her. "You speak it poorly, but I can understand you."

"What's he saying?" Aaron asked.

Jennifer replied in English without taking her eyes off the samurai. "Nothing important, yet. He's saying that I speak the language poorly."

"Maybe it's different time periods," Aaron said. "You studied modern Japanese. These guys don't exactly look like they're from the twentieth century."

"I don't know much about Japan," Travis said, "but I know guns. Their weapons are matchlocks. See the burning fuses wrapped around their left forearms? Those guns are really primitive."

Otomo spoke again, pointing at the corpses. His voice was deep and angry.

"What's he want?" Aaron asked.

"He wants to know why we killed those men," Jennifer translated.

"Tell him we didn't do it," Aaron said.

He watched the samurai's face closely as Jennifer spoke. Otomo, still frowning, looked unconvinced.

"Tell him," Aaron said, "that we're chasing the man who did. Tell him our enemy killed his men."

Jennifer relayed Aaron's words. Otomo seemed to consider them, then questioned Jennifer.

"He wants to know," Jennifer said, "who our enemy is and why he is our enemy."

"Eckels," Travis spit out in a voice as harsh as the samurai's.

Aaron nodded. "Yes. The man's name is Eckels." He hesitated. It would only damage what little credibility they had, Aaron thought, if he started to rave about time travel and alternate histories. On the other hand, he didn't want just to make things up. They had to get along with these samurai. He couldn't tell a story now that would be indefensible later. He decided to stick to the truth, but to keep it simple. "Eckels stole something of ours. Something very valuable that we need back."

Otomo grunted and nodded noncommittally after Jennifer had translated this. He turned to Katsu, who, Jennifer noticed, was on his knees, his head bowed to the ground. They conversed swiftly for a few minutes.

"He's asking Katsu what happened," Jennifer said. "Katsu is confirming that we didn't kill these men and that we're from the Land Beyond the Stone."

Otomo grunted and nodded. He spoke to Jennifer in a softer, less demanding voice.

"He's inviting us to their castle to meet his lord, his *daimyo*."

"We should go after Eckels," Travis said.

"I think it's really more of an order than an invitation, though he's being polite about it."

"We should find out more about the local situation before we poke our noses into it," Aaron said.

Travis acquiesced with a grunt.

Mundo, seeing that things were calming down, stepped out into the open for the first time. A whisper of astonishment rippled through the ranks of the foot soldiers. Even Otomo seemed surprised and impressed. He pointed at Mundo and shot off a few questions. To his obvious astonishment, Mundo answered him in Japanese.

"What now?" Aaron asked.

"He wanted to know to whom the monkey belonged," Mundo said with a sniff. "I told him that I'm not a monkey and that I belong to no one."

Otomo spoke again. Mundo gave a monkeylike smile and nodded. He answered at some length.

"What was that about?" Aaron asked.

"Oh, he just told me that I spoke much better than the woman. Of course, I told him."

It seemed to Aaron that the conversation had been longer than that. He realized, as the foot soldiers formed ranks around them that were as much a cage as an escort of honor, that Mundo might speak the language better than Jennifer, but they couldn't fully trust him.

They had to remember that he was an alien creature with his own agenda. And that agenda might not always mesh with theirs.

6

Strangers in a Strange Land

SStragh hesitated only briefly, but by the time she followed Eikels's killing-thing onto the Floating Stone and crossed over into the other world, a handful of seconds had gone by.

The killing-thing was no longer in sight, but evidence of its passing was all around. It had broken down a wall of the human structure which enclosed the Floating Stone. Three humans lay bloody and battered. They were twisted and broken without mark of spear or club on them, slain by the same far-killer that had accounted for so many Mutata lately.

SStragh leaned over one of the corpses and sniffed gently. Though the stench of death lay over it like a concealing shroud, she could still recognize the scent. It smelled like the armored humans who had come into the Mutata valley to kill without proper warning or challenge.

Outwardly, it looked a lot like Jhenini and Peeitah, but its scent was very different. It ate different things, wore different-smelling clothing, used different oils on its hair and skin. Though it had the basic human smell, its individual scent was very different.

SStragh looked up alertly. Her sensitive nostrils detected another human. This one was still alive. The symphony of odors it gave off was somewhere between that of Jhenini and these other humans, if closer to the humans of this place.

SStragh whirled, changing her spear to the left hand, the proper hand, and issued the challenge. She knew that the human was behind a thicket on the side of the clearing. She snorted her challenge again, her crest erect along the back of her head, its color deepening into a lush, emerald green.

For a moment nothing happened. Then a tiny spear catapulted out of the covering shrubbery, moving so fast that SStragh knew she had no chance to dodge it. But it flew harmlessly by her head, missing by a scant inch. The unexpected attack was startling, but SStragh wasn't hurt. The enormity of the insult, though, almost left her speechless with anger.

To be hunted from ambush like some brainless beast! She honked in stuttering rage.

She transferred her spear to her right hand almost unconsciously and charged the thicket with her nostrils flared in anger. She burst through the screening shrubbery to see that the human hiding there had already taken flight. He was running quickly through the forest at a speed that SStragh couldn't hope to match.

SStragh watched him go, her anger fading as suddenly as it had arisen. She didn't understand these humans. She doubted that she ever would. Perhaps according to their life-path, this ambush was not the enormous insult it would have been according to the OColihi, the Mutata worldview.

She of all people should consider that possibility, for she was one of the few who believed that the OColihi should be adapted to the Mutatas' current needs.

Perhaps, SStragh considered. But attacking from ambush without issuing the proper challenges would never be part of her OColihi.

SStragh looked around, realizing for the first time the strangeness of her surroundings. It was abnormally quiet. There seemed to be no sounds in this strange forest. The air was dry, so dry that it irritated her throat when she breathed. And the smells! Or, more correctly, lack of smells, was almost overpowering. It was a dull, dry, almost colorless place when compared to her world.

A small creature suddenly flitted by. It was a flying lizard, but oddly enough was covered entirely in dull brown feathers. There was no pebbly hide of beautiful iridescent colors, only a boring blend of brown, white, and black. There seemed to be little life in this forest, and what life existed seemed rather colorless.

Even the plants were different. Hesitantly she reached out, bending a branch down to her lips. She broke off a few leaves, chewed them carefully, and spit them out. They had no flavor, and probably no nourishment. She wondered how long she'd be able to survive in this strange world.

SStragh turned back to the clearing and looked wistfully at the structure that housed the Floating Stone. She could go back to her world. She could go back and get Jhenini. Together they could hunt Eikels in this new world.

But this was not Jhenini's task. Eikels had killed SStragh's tribesmen from the shelter of his shell. It was her job, not Jhenini's, to exact payment for those deaths.

The trail clearly led deeper into the forest. SStragh could see the marks it left as it passed through the wood and smell the strange sharp scent of it. She followed it into a forest like no other she had ever known.

It was almost like coming home again, though Aaron remembered that his last homecoming had turned into something of a nightmare.

They strolled through an oak and maple forest just like the one that surrounded Green Town. The landscape was so familiar that Aaron could even place exactly where they were—perhaps a quarter-mile from his house, farther south in the woods. There seemed to be no buildings anywhere, no sign of man except for the dirt trail that led in the general direction of Green Town.

"This is so familiar," Jennifer whispered. "So much like home."

"Only it's not home," Aaron reminded her.

"In some ways it looks better." They walked on in silence for a moment, then Jennifer added, "Aren't we going right by where your house should be?"

"So you recognized the spot too?"

They passed by the Cofield house site. Only in this world there was no house, no barn, no driveway, no lawn. There were no plowed fields, no Green Town visible in the distance. This was virgin Illinois, only lightly touched by the hands of men. Only when they had reached where Green Town somewhere slumbered near the banks of the Ohio River did they see more extensive signs of man.

Tall earthworks enclosed what would have been downtown Green Town in Aaron's world. The earthworks were like great dikes holding back a rippling sea that was hundreds of acres of flooded rice paddies. The earthen walls were about ten feet high and four feet across, their apparent height increased by the dry moat before them. There was one gate in the earthen barrier. It was guarded by armed samurai. A host of people worked in the paddies, apparently weeding the rice plants. The workers seemed to be both Japanese and American Indians. There were a few thatched cottages outside the earthworks, but no elaborate buildings.

The guards at the gate saluted them through without batting an eye. Inside the palisade were fifty or more thatched cottages that were a little bigger, a little more elaborate than those outside the enclosure. There was also a corral with a couple dozen horses lazing about and what looked like a small mill located on the bank of a creek that ran through the center of the enclosure.

The settlement was dominated by a single large building that sat behind interior fortifications on the highest point of ground in the enclosure. It was the settlement's citadel. This citadel was sturdily built of timber and stone rather than thatch.

"Looks like a fort of some kind," Travis said.

"Maybe all the Indians in the area aren't as friendly as the ones we've seen so far," Aaron said. "Maybe there's a war going on."

"And we've been taken prisoner," Jennifer added.

"Just as long as they feed us some decent food," Peter said. "I'm starving."

Aaron, too, realized that he was hungry. Eating had been catch-as-catch-can over the last few days, and at Peter's mention of food his stomach started to grumble.

The citadel's portal was also guarded. They stopped before the plank bridge that ran over the dry moat and Otomo dismissed his unit. He said a few words to the men on sentry duty. One saluted, turned, and ran into the keep ahead of them. They followed and the captain signaled a stop in the dim, cool anteroom.

"What are we waiting for?" Jennifer asked.

He looked down at her haughtily. "I have sent word ahead for servants to come so that you may be properly greeted as guests. You will be brought before my master, Lord Akira Yoshinori." He sniffed delicately. "When you have been properly . . . prepared."

Jennifer nodded and translated for the benefit of the others. In a few moments two groups of servants appeared. Both squads bowed deeply before the samurai and looked up, somewhat skeptically, at the others. Particularly Mundo.

"If you will follow them, please." Otomo's words were polite, but his tone indicated it was more of an order than a request.

A female servant bowed to Jennifer and started to lead her away from the others.

"Hey, wait a minute," Aaron protested. "She stays with us."

Otomo didn't understand Aaron's words, but he understood the tone that Aaron used. He glared at Aaron, who glared back.

"Don't start anything foolish," Jennifer said.

"But you can't go off by yourself—"

"I've been by myself for some time, now," she said sharply. "I can manage. It's obvious that they want us to bathe and change our clothes. They would be shocked, I'm sure, if you told them we all wanted to bathe together."

Aaron nodded sheepishly. "I guess you're right. Still, I don't want to be separated from you again."

Jennifer laid a hand on his arm. "I don't want that either. But I'm sure it will be only for a short time. We've been well-treated so far. Why would that change?"

"You never know," Peter put in darkly.

"I appreciate your concern," Jennifer said with a smile. "But I can take care of myself."

"I'm sure you can," Aaron said.

Otomo followed this exchange with lively, silent interest. When it was finished he spoke a few quick sentences to Jennifer in a tone that was softer and more reserved than he'd used before. He then bowed slightly toward Jennifer, nodded really, a bare millimeter or two.

Jennifer responded with an ever-so-slightly deeper bow, and a single phrase, "*Domo arigato*."

"What was all that?" Aaron asked.

"Captain Otomo says not to worry, that we are his honored guests."

"He means it, too," Mundo piped up. "I can't hear any treachery in him."

Aaron nodded. "Tell him thank you. Thank you very much."

As Mundo translated, Aaron bowed as Jennifer had. The captain bowed his precise millimeter in return. His hard, unblinking gaze never left them as they followed the servants down the corridor. Aaron resisted the impulse to look back over his shoulder, wishing that he could read minds like Mundo.

He would give anything to know what Otomo was really thinking.

7

A Hot Bath, Good Food, and Startling Information

"What is this," Peter asked, "a swimming pool?"

It was a rhetorical question, since there was no one present capable of answering him. The servants had conducted them through the citadel and out a back door that opened onto a beautifully tended garden. There were flowering plants everywhere, even in the garden pool which was also home to a number of large, colorful fish. A trail of square flagstones led across the emerald green lawn to a small building that was screened from view by a grove of tall, thickly planted bamboo plants. The servants opened the door, which was actually a sliding frame of translucent paper, bowed them into the structure, and left.

Aaron squatted before the pool. He could feel heat coming off the water. "They probably want us to take a bath. The Japanese are pretty big on communal baths."

"What, together?" Peter asked.

"You were never afraid to take showers after gym class, were you?" Aaron said. "As for me, I could use a good soak."

"So can I," Travis said. He stripped off clothes stained with blood, sweat, and the grime of several different time-lines. He dropped them into a sloppy pile and eased himself into the pool. He let out a long, satisfied sigh as the warm water closed over his bruised and battered body. "Ahh, that feels good."

Aaron joined him, then Peter. Mundo looked at the water dubiously. He stuck a toe in.

"Ah, I don't think they meant for you to take a bath, Mundo," Aaron said. "Wet fur smells pretty bad, you know."

Mundo retreated from the water. "No, I didn't. I'll take your word for it, though. This body doesn't seem to be eager to jump into the water anyway."

The paper sliding door slipped open quietly. Katsu was kneeling outside the bathhouse. He quickly said a few hushed sentences as he bowed low, his face almost on the ground.

Mundo translated. "He says Otomo has assigned him to be our servant while we're guests here."

"Well, tell the boy to come in," Travis said. "We got some questions to ask him. Besides, he's letting in cool air."

After Mundo finished translating, Katsu nodded once and said "*Hai.*"

He rose from his knees, turned, stepped over the threshold of the bathhouse, knelt again with his back to the room's interior, and picked up the pile of towels he had left outside the room. Then he slid the door shut and finally turned and faced the others.

"Well," Aaron said to Mundo, "talk to him. Get some information out of him. I hate operating in the dark."

"Sure," Mundo said. "No problem."

Katsu was a willing and loquacious informant. Mundo had to speak quickly to keep up with the words spilling from him.

"My village," Katsu said, "is the easternmost settlement in the domain of Lord Akira Tomiko, *Daimyo* of the Endless Lands. There are two great *daimyos* in this new land that we, the Nipponjin—the people of Nippon—had discovered over a hundred years ago. Shushen Itiyama holds the Coastal Territory and the land to the Great Mountains. Lord Akira Tomiko is *daimyo* of the plains east of the mountains, which are called the Endless Lands.

"Our expansion into the Endless Lands has been limited so far by the ferocity of the local savages, who are much more belligerent than those who live on the coast. There are many different groups of these savages, but only three main types. The Roamers live on the Great Plains and follow the great herds of wild, shaggy cows. The Hill Makers live in villages among the great river valleys. Finally, tribes to the east call themselves Iroquois."

"The Roamers must be Plains Indians," Aaron interjected, "and the Hill Makers must be the culture we call the Mound Builders."

"I knew that," Peter told him.

"There are few Nipponjin settlements on the Great Plains," Katsu continued. "We rarely deal with the Roamers because we live near river valleys where we can grow rice. Some of the Roamers are hostile, but others have allied themselves with my lord.

"The Hill Makers are a different matter." Katsu frowned as he spoke of them. "They too prefer to live in the river valleys where they build permanent villages centered around their handmade hills of earth. The Hill Makers are more civilized than the Roamers. They live in one place all year round and plant and tend crops. But in some ways they are even more savage than the Roamers. A terrible god has arisen among them who demands awful sacrifices.

"We have fought with them ever since we came to this place. There's sure to be trouble between us in coming years." But Katsu wasn't frightened of them, believing that the Hill Maker warriors were no match for the steel of the samurai or the matchlocks of the *ashigaru*, the commoner foot soldiers.

Katsu shook his head when Aaron interrupted to ask about the Iroquois, a name familiar to him from history books.

There were no Nipponjin settlements in Iroquois territory, Katsu told him. In fact, only the bravest samurai have ever returned from scouting missions into their country. The Iroquois are the most warlike of the natives. The Nipponjin didn't know much about them except that they knew the art of agriculture, lived in permanent settlements most of the year, and were the fiercest fighters on the continent. Besides the samurai of Lord Akira, of course. The Iroquois were so savage that they frequently ate the people they vanquished.

Katsu could understand the concept of taking heads—all great warlords took the heads of their enemies after defeating them in battle. But eating their foes? Katsu shook his head. That was beyond his comprehension.

The Iroquois had already devastated several of the tribes who had once lived near them. Those tribes had either been wiped out or had moved away and relinquished their territory to the Iroquois. Worst of all, some tribes had became slaves of their conquerors.

The Iroquois were also pushing into the territory of the Hill Makers. There had been battles between the tribes, but the warring groups had declared a truce since the Nipponjin had moved into the region. "Perhaps," Katsu said, "they are planning on joining forces against the outsiders." No one really knew.

The Nipponjin village had been here for six years, Katsu told them. During this time relations between the Nipponjin and the various native peoples had ground to an impasse. The native tribes hadn't been able to drive the Nipponjin off the land, but neither had the Nipponjin gone deeper into their territory. The biggest loss to the village had been the death of their headman the year before in a Hill Maker ambush. In response to this loss, Akira Tomiko had sent his younger brother, Akira Yoshinori, to be the new headman for the region.

"This is fascinating," Aaron said. "For some reason the Europeans never made it to the New World in this timeline. At least not permanently or in large numbers. Apparently the Japanese crossed the Pacific and are colonizing America themselves."

"Yeah," Peter said, stifling a yawn. "In the meantime I'm turning into a prune. I'm getting out of here." He paused, looking distastefully at his filthy T-shirt and jeans. "I'd sure hate to put those on again after finally getting clean."

"I know what you mean," Travis said. "I could use some fresh clothes myself."

"Mundo—" Aaron began.

"I know, I know. Ask the kid."

"While you're at it, ask about some food."

"Yeah." Mundo scratched his hairy stomach. "I could use a banana or two myself."

"*Hai*," Katsu said, bowing low. "Other servants are bringing you fresh clothing that we will be honored if you wear while yours is . . . laundered." Katsu, glancing at the piles of dirty clothes, was apparently of the opinion that incineration would be a more suitable fate for them. "Lord Akira wishes to meet you. He prays for you to join him at the midday rice."

"Sounds good," Travis said. "I'm hungry enough to eat—" he fell silent as he thought it over "—almost anything."

He started to get out of the water, then the paper sliding door slipped open again. Two maids bearing bundles of clothing knelt outside the bathhouse.

"Hey," Travis said, sliding back into the water up to his neck.

Katsu looked at him, perplexed.

"The kid wants to know what's wrong," Mundo translated.

"Nothing," Travis said, red from more than the heat of the bath. "Just bring the clothes in and get rid of the women."

"Won't you require their assistance in dressing?" Katsu wanted to know.

"I've been dressing myself for a long time, sonny. I don't need any help."

Aaron and Peter laughed, but both were also glad when Katsu took the bundles of clothing and the maids bowed themselves out of the bathhouse.

"We're in a tricky spot," Aaron said. "This is a truly alien culture. We'll have to watch ourselves to make sure we don't get into any trouble."

"What's this?" Travis asked, holding up an article of clothing that looked something like a large jockstrap.

"*Fundoshi*," Katsu said, correctly interpreting Travis's question. He made motions of stepping into it and pulling it up around his waist.

"I guess that's what passes for underwear around here," Aaron said, putting on a pair. Then he held up a pair of short trousers that were so wide in the leg that they looked like culottes.

"*Hakama*," Katsu said.

"Right." Aaron put them on, trying the drawstring so that they wouldn't immediately fall down around his ankles again.

He picked up a third garment. It was a kimono, made from a rich, silky fabric. The coloring was a dark, soft brown. There were patches of color, round badges, on the back and on the front and also on the wide sleeves. They were the same badges they'd seen on Captain Otomo and his men, the red sun emblazoned upon a pure white background.

Katsu, meanwhile, was collecting their clothing, trying not to wrinkle his nose too obviously at their ripe odor. He'd just gathered them into a single pile when the door to the bathhouse slid open again. This time there were no bowing maids. Captain Otomo stooped slightly to enter the bathhouse and regarded Aaron and the others with his hard, hawklike stare. Otomo was dressed in *hakama* and a simple, but elegantly cut, kimono tied at the waist with a red sash. Aaron remembered that Katsu had said the red sash was a badge of honor given to those samurai who had crossed over to the Land Beyond the Stone. Otomo was apparently brave and capable as well as stern.

Aaron glanced at Katsu. The servant boy was kneeling on the floor, his head pressed to the ground. Aaron suddenly knew what Otomo was waiting for. He bowed, inclining his head until he looked at the floor. Travis followed him after a moment, then Peter, after Aaron had jabbed him in the ribs with his elbow. Otomo, seemingly satisfied at last, bowed his sharp, precise millimeter, and the others all looked up.

"How come the monkey doesn't have to bow to his highness?" Peter complained.

"That's Monkey *King* to you," Mundo said haughtily.

"I suspect," Aaron said slowly, "because he's unique. He's unlike anything they've ever seen, so they don't know where he fits in the social order."

"That's right," Mundo said smugly. "I'm one of a kind. You're just people but they're not quite sure of you either. You're obviously not samurai, because you don't dress like samurai or wear your hair like samurai or carry two swords like samurai. Yet you've come through the magic portal from the Land Beyond the Stone. And you have a rifle."

Aaron and Travis both looked at Mundo.

"Oh yes, these people aren't fools. They recognize a rifle when they see one. And they know what one can do. They know that their men at the shrine were gunned down. So they're being cautious. Oh yes, very cautious."

Otomo waited patiently with no expression at all on his face as Mundo explained the things he'd skimmed from the samurai's mind. When Mundo finished, Otomo spoke shortly, politely, and to the point, punctuating his speech with a wave of his arm, indicating that everyone was to leave the bathhouse.

"Now that we're all tidied up," Mundo said, "it seems we've been invited to lunch."

"About time," Peter said. "I'm starved."

For once Aaron agreed with him. It had been a long time since he had eaten at the Cofield house in that strange, altered Green Town that was so similar—yet so utterly alien—to his own.

Otomo led the procession back into the citadel's main building. Aaron, Peter, and Travis followed. Katsu brought up the rear and Mundo capered from the front of the group to the back as the mood grabbed him. Katsu disappeared somewhere inside the keep before they went through a final door and entered the audience chamber of Lord Akira Yoshinori.

It was a large, open room. There was no furniture, other than a small table on short legs which Lord Akira, magnificent in his brocaded kimono, leaned against. The floor of Akira's end of the room was higher than the area where Aaron and the others knelt.

Otomo immediately bowed as low to the ground as the servants had bowed to him. Aaron and the others followed Otomo's lead immediately—except for Mundo who stood upright, frowning and scratching his hairy stomach. Akira took no notice of them for several long moments. Instead, he seemed intent on whatever was contained in one of several small vessels set atop the little table against which he leaned. He was engrossed in what looked like a stick of burning incense, his eyes closed, his cheeks twitching as he took short, sharp sniffs. Later Aaron discovered that Akira was taking part in one of his favorite hobbies: incense appreciation. It was an aesthetic tradition very popular in the Imperial Court in Nippon, though here at the edge of the Endless Lands it was regarded as one of the Lord's odd little peccadilloes.

Lord Akira finally looked up and said a languid word. Otomo answered, but remained bowed, his forehead pressed against the mat that covered the wooden floor. Mundo strutted to the front of the room. Lord Akira's eyebrows rose in astonishment when Mundo addressed him in his own language.

"Greetings, oh great Lord, Master of all you survey."

"You speak?" Akira said. "You speak our language?"

"Of course, Lord," Mundo replied. "Of what use to you would I be otherwise?"

"How remarkable," Akira said in polite understatement. "To what do we owe the pleasure of this meeting?"

Mundo then launched into a long, barely coherent summary of events which stuck fairly close to the truth, if exaggerating somewhat his importance and position in them. Akira seemed fascinated. Aaron, who of course couldn't understand a word of what either was saying, couldn't tell if it was Mundo's story or Mundo himself that captivated Lord Akira.

Finally, after what must have been fifteen minutes, when Aaron's thighs were starting to scream with the steady ache of the unaccustomed bowing position, Mundo finished his story and Lord Akira seemed to notice the rest of them.

"How remarkable," Akira said again. Aaron was to find that that was one of Akira's favorite phrases. Sometimes he applied it to the most unremarkable things.

Akira spoke another phrase and gestured. Otomo arose and joined Akira on the dais, sitting at his right hand.

"You may rise," Otomo said.

Mundo translated. They sat up, but remained kneeling in an uncomfortable position on the floor. At least the mats which padded the wooden floor were soft.

Akira spoke again.

"Our guests are hungry," Mundo said, translating the Lord's words. Akira didn't look at them as he spoke. It seemed as if he were speaking to the air, but the door panel behind him slid open and a gorgeously kimonoed woman placed a covered tray on the floor of the audience chamber. She got up from a kneeling position outside the room, crossed the threshold, knelt again, and then slid the door shut. She served Akira the tray. Moments later, another went through the same complicated process and brought a tray for Otomo. Behind her were four other maids, bearing trays for each of Akira's guests.

They also brought in little tables upon which they set the trays. Peter uncovered his. The food looked and smelled unfamiliar, but good. He reached for the chopsticks.

"Aren't we forgetting something?" Aaron said, leaving his tray untouched.

"What?" Peter asked.

"Jennifer. Where is she?"

Mundo put the question to Akira, who looked vaguely astonished.

"This is men's business," Akira said. "She is being taken care of appropriately. Do not worry."

Aaron couldn't help but worry, but he knew better than to push things. The food was unfamiliar but delicious. The first serving seemed to be hors d'oeuvres of various types. Tiny bits of meat and fish were served with spiced vegetables and wrapped balls of rice. Sushi deluxe. After they had polished off the last morsel, heaping bowls of steaming white rice were brought out. Everyone was hungry enough to eat everything, even Mundo, who entertained Akira with his quips and anecdotes as he ate.

It wasn't long before Aaron was really wishing that Jennifer was present to translate what Mundo was saying. He seemed to be entertaining Lord Akira, but Otomo knelt before his table like the original stone face, eating sparingly and saying little.

"Mundo's turning into quite the raconteur, isn't he?" Travis said quietly.

Aaron glanced at him. "You noticed it too?"

"How couldn't I? He hasn't shut up since we entered the audience chamber."

"Is that unusual?" Peter asked.

"Yeah. I wonder why he's so chatty all of a sudden."

"It's obvious," Peter said. "He's sucking up. He knows who's the lord high muckety-muck around here and wants to make sure he gets in with him."

Travis and Aaron looked at each other.

"Think so?" Travis asked.

"Maybe. When we get the chance we'd better remind him that we're all in this together."

"I'll remind him," Travis promised with tight lips.

Just as the final dishes were being cleared away by the maids a samurai burst into the audience room. He prostrated himself on the floor, excitedly rattling off a message that brought Akira to his feet.

"What did he say?" Aaron asked Mundo.

"Apparently," the ape said, "a dragon has been sighted by Akira's spies in Hill Maker territory. A two-legged dragon carrying a spear. They say it's been captured by the savages."

"It must be Jennifer's friend, SStragh," Aaron said.

It was then, as Akira stood, that Aaron for the first time could see the gorgeous pattern that was emblazoned across the front and the back of the lord's silken kimono.

It was a dragon, a two-legged dragon that looked so much like a Mutata that it could have been modeled from life.

8

Captured

Eckels slammed his fist against the time machine's control panel in frustration, doing nothing more constructive than causing a sharp pain to run up his forearm to his elbow.

The blasted machine simply wouldn't work. Oh, it would putter around, but ultimately that was of little utility. A check of the fuel gauge told him that soon even this bit of usefulness would come to an end.

Eckels couldn't understand why the machine refused to move in time. He wasn't an expert in temporal mechanics, certainly, but then neither were low-class outdoorsmen like Travis. Eckels had piloted temporal craft before. Sure, he might have made a mistake or two, but he had always been able to move about easily enough. Now that he had got free of that cursed reptilian world, he was certain that he would be able to find his way back home.

If only the machine would work.

A grumbling sound deep within his stomach distracted him from his futile attempts to get the time machine to function. He stood up and stretched, realizing he'd spent several futile hours huddled over the controls.

He was hungry and thirsty. The machine carried no provisions, but there were several weapons racked in place on the wall. And Eckels was a hunter. He could provide for himself, that was certain, if this timeline had anything better to offer in the way of game than miserable little rats and feathered lizards.

First things first, though. This machine was his new cave. Only it was more familiar, comfortable, and safe than any hole in the ground. Unfortunately, it was also more visible. He had to find a secure place to stash it in case those people he'd run into when he had first shifted into this world should come looking for him.

Well, Eckels smiled, not those *exact* people. He'd taken care of them all right. They'd tried to swarm all over him when he'd shifted into this reality. He'd been safe in the time craft, but he didn't want any witnesses to his arrival, witnesses who could follow him, who could put God knows how many others onto his trail. He'd had to take care of them, and he did, quick as that. Their puny swords had been no match for automatic rifles designed to stop the biggest, dumbest dinosaur.

Eckels scanned the area. There didn't seem to be any especially terrific spots where he could safely stash the machine. Still, some cover was better than none.

He carefully maneuvered the machine into a deep thicket of brambles that was partially screened by a fallen tree. At least this world had proper plants in it. That probably meant proper animals, too. Eckels's mouth watered at the thought of a steak carved from some large, beefy mammal. *Although,* he told himself, *even a rabbit or two would be good.*

No squirrels, though. Skinned, they reminded him too much of the unsavory rodents that had formed the basis of his diet in that damned dinosaur world.

He exited the time craft, carefully climbing through the berry-loaded bushes that were prickly with sharp thorns. He rearranged the bushes as best he could, deciding that after he'd tracked down something and eaten, he'd cut some brush to camouflage the front of the craft. With that done he would have a pretty snug hideout.

Eckels was standing with his rifle slung over his back by its carrying strap and his hands on his hips when he heard an ungodly roar so close behind him that he jumped with fright.

He came down in a crouch, half turned, and looked behind him. He stared in disbelief. It was one of those blasted dinosaurs. Most of those scaly creatures looked alike to Eckels, but he did recognize this one. It was the one who always hung around the compound where they'd been imprisoned, the one with whom Jennifer had spent hours talking—if you could call the hoots, roars, and whistles they exchanged talking.

Eckels felt an immediate sense of dislocation—what was it *doing* here?—immediately followed by a wave of persecution. It had followed him. It had to have followed him into this new time-stream. But why?

Whatever reasons it had, Eckels thought, the thing was angry. He'd been around the big lizards long enough to recognize when one of them had a mad on, and this one was furious.

Its mottled skin had vivid patches of deep emerald green. The crest that ran atop its head and down the back of its spine was erect. Most importantly, it had a spear in its hand which it waved menacingly at Eckels as it roared another challenge.

"I know you," Eckels told it. "You're the lizard who palled around with Jennifer. You think you're pretty tough." Eckels unslung the rifle and pointed it at SStragh. "You know what this is, don't you?"

SStragh's gaze flickered from Eckels's face, down to the rifle he held, and back again. She uttered another challenge and hopped forward mincingly, drawing her spear back even further.

"You do know what it is," Eckels said. "But it's not going to stop you, is it? And I thought you lizards were supposed to be smart. Bye-bye."

Eckels smiled, but before he could pull the trigger a series of hair-raising ululating cries gave him pause. He looked around in bewilderment, at first thinking that SStragh had unseen allies who were just now making themselves known.

But SStragh, he saw, was just as bewildered as he. The creature lowered her spear, and peered around uncertainly as if she, too, was unsure what the sounds meant.

"Now what?" Eckels asked plaintively.

He didn't have long to wait. A commanding voice called out from the cover of the woods. The language was unknown to Eckels, who had a nodding familiarity with a number of tongues. This one, however, sounded like nothing he had ever heard.

In a moment, as if in response to the commands shouted in the unknown language, a band of men broke from the cover of the woods. There were twenty or thirty of them. Eckels might have been able to handle that many with his automatic rifle if they were standing around in a single clump, but they had spread out under cover. They remained spread out as they stepped into the open. Besides, most of them carried primitive-looking, but nonetheless probably effective, projectile weapons called bows and arrows.

Not only did their weapons look primitive, but so did the men themselves. They were scantily dressed in hide clothing, mostly skirtlike kilts. Most were shirtless. Some had painted or tattooed faces, Eckels couldn't be sure which, and most had feather ornaments stuck in their long black hair.

They were not at all like the men Eckels had crossed paths with earlier. These were a different cultural group, probably even a different race entirely. Eckels was no history expert, but it seemed to him that they might be what was known as Indians, a primitive tribal-based culture that had been extinct by Eckels's time.

Well, at least they were men and not lizards.

Eckels stood slowly, a big grin on his face.

"Am I glad to see you," he said enthusiastically. "Not that I couldn't handle things myself, but you'll make things even easier." He pointed at SStragh. "Kill that thing," he said. "Go ahead, kill it. It doesn't belong here."

SStragh reacted calmly to the sudden appearance of the newcomers. She had backed down from her posture of attack. Her spear was by her side, her color faded considerably from the virulent green it had been a few moments before. She was regarding the newcomers with hooded, tranquil eyes, but you never knew, Eckels thought, what was going on in what passed for a lizard's brain.

The newcomers seemed quite taken with SStragh. There was a degree of acceptance to their attitude which surprised Eckels. The first time he'd seen a talking two-legged lizard it had scared the bejesus out of him. If he'd had the drop on it, he would have snuffed it immediately.

Only the Indians weren't reacting that way. They kept their weapons out and ready, but they were talking animatedly about SStragh. While they kept an eye on Eckels, they were for the most part shooting awed glances at the reptilian monstrosity, who also seemed to be taking things with great equanimity.

These people, Eckels realized, had either seen or heard about two-legged lizards before. Maybe, Eckels thought, SStragh wasn't the first one to step on the temporal roadway and end up here.

"Look guys," Eckels said, waving his rifle for emphasis, "if you don't want to take care of ugly here, I will."

As he raised his weapon to his cheek and aimed at SStragh, a storm of angry shouts came from the forest. The Indians' attention switched immediately to Eckels, and he suddenly found himself the focal point of thirty poised arrows. Cursing silently to himself, he slowly lowered his weapon.

The Indians, though, kept theirs pointed.

There was more rattling in the bushes and four more of the savages pushed into the clearing. Three of the newcomers were large and muscular. They appeared to be the personal guards of the fourth.

This last was older than the others, though he still looked as if he had a few good years left. His age showed in the streaks of gray which ran through his glossy black hair. He was big and strong-looking, with muscular arms and a broad chest. He had no ready weapons, though he did carry a sword sheathed at his side. He was solemn-looking, with an air of command about him that was intensified by the dark designs tattooed on his face. The tattoos made his face look like a bird of prey.

He glanced at SStragh, who still stood silently and patiently, watching closely all that was happening. Then, followed by his retinue of bodyguards, he came up to Eckels. He stopped and pointed at the rifle Eckels had cradled in his arm.

When Eckels did nothing he pointed again, more insistently.

Eckels looked at him. His eyes were hard. There was no playing around with this guy.

"Gun," Eckels said, holding it out. "Rifle."

Gray Hair, as Eckels thought of him, pantomimed putting a rifle to his shoulder and pulling the trigger.

Eckels nodded. "That's right. Rifle."

Solemn-faced, Gray Hair also nodded. Then he reached out quickly and smoothly took the rifle from Eckels. He was so fast and so strong that Eckels couldn't even offer token resistance.

"Hey," Eckels said. He started forward, but so did the three bodyguards. Two of them had long, shiny metal knives. A third had what looked like a club with a large knob at the end carved out of some hard wood. It was a graceful, but lethal-looking, weapon. Eckels backed away and pasted a smile on his face.

"Sure, take it," he said with as much friendliness as he could muster.

Gray Hair nodded once. He put the rifle to his shoulder, sighted high at the trees surrounding them, and pulled the trigger. The result was immediate and devastating. A line of slugs ripped through the trees, shattering good-sized branches and chopping through a few smaller trunks. A murmur rose up among the savages. Even the otherwise imperturbable Gray Hair looked startled. He brought the gun down, looked at it closely, and said a few words, half to himself.

Finally he looked at Eckels. In one swift move he drew the sword that was sheathed at his side. Eckels cringed backward, evoking a few chuckles from Gray Hair's bodyguards.

But the Indian didn't try to stick Eckels. Instead, he extended the sword hilt first and made a gesture as if Eckels should take it. Eckels looked from the sword, to Gray Hair's face, then nodded.

"I get it. You want to trade."

Gray Hair made another commanding gesture and Eckels reluctantly accepted the sword.

"I wouldn't exactly call it a fair trade," Eckels grumbled. "But what can I do about it? It's a good thing there's a few more rifles in the machine."

Gray Hair handed the weapon to one of his bodyguards and all three studied it closely, muttering wonderingly over it. Gray Hair looked steadily at Eckels, then pointed at SStragh and gestured questioningly.

"What do you want me to say?" Eckels asked. "It's a big lizard."

Gray Hair looked back at Eckels, then nodded decisively. He made a commanding gesture for Eckels to follow him.

"You're the boss."

They went over to the warriors who still surrounded SStragh. The lizard looked cool and unconcerned, at least as far as Eckels could tell. Gray Hair caught its attention and talked at it for some length. It stood still as a statue, its gold-flecked eyes unblinking. When Gray Hair finished speaking at SStragh he turned and looked questioningly at Eckels.

"What do you want from me?" Eckels asked, fighting to keep the irritation out of his voice. "I can't understand the thing either."

Gray Hair seemed to understand the substance, if not the exact meaning, of Eckels's words. He made a roundup gesture with his right hand and, still flanked by his bodyguards, turned and suddenly started for the woods again.

A couple of the warriors who had been watching the lizard turned their attention to Eckels. One pointed with his spear, aiming it at Eckels's midsection.

"Okay, I get the idea. You don't have to stab me."

Eckels fell in line, following Gray Hair and his bodyguards back into the forest. He glanced back over his shoulder, wondering if SStragh would get the point and follow the script. She did. The warriors circling her peeled off slowly and SStragh unhesitatingly found a place in the procession. The blasted thing was pretty smart, Eckels admitted to himself.

Once they reached the cover of the woods they joined up with the rest of the party. Two additional warriors were guarding five prisoners, whose hands were tied behind their backs and whose ankles were hobbled. These men also looked like warriors. They still wore armor, but their weapons had been taken away from them. They were dressed differently from Gray Hair's group, obviously belonging to the faction that Eckels had run into when he'd first crossed into this timeline.

The prisoners had apparently just been in a desperate fight. They all were disheveled and had cuts and scratches, but two seemed more severely injured. One had taken an arrow in the chest; the other had a bad gash on his right thigh. Both wounds were bandaged, but both were still seeping blood. Their fellow prisoners helped the injured along as best they could as they resumed the march through the forest.

Eckels wondered what his status was as they went along the trail at a fairly good clip. It obviously wasn't as low as that of the bound prisoners. He was unfettered and, although he'd been relieved of his rifle, his captors had allowed him to keep the sword Gray Hair had forced on him in exchange. On the other hand, the two men marching at his back were keeping a very close watch on him. If he wasn't a captive, it was evident that he wasn't exactly an honored guest, either.

Infrequent backward glances told him that his guards were alert and attentive. It wouldn't do, he decided, to try to make a dash for it. Not only did the Indians obviously know the terrain better than he did, they looked like they were in excellent shape. Eckels knew they would run him down in moments if he tried to make a break.

They had treated him all right so far. They'd kept the big lizard from attacking him, though he probably could have handled the spear-chucking reptile with ease. He would likely get some decent food at their village, maybe take it easy for a day or two. And then, well fed and rested, he'd sneak away, head back to the time machine, and figure out why the blazes it wasn't working right.

All he had to do was stay alert, take it easy, and look for his chance. There was no way he couldn't outwit these savages and make his escape when the opportunity presented itself.

The forest became more open, turning into sparsely treed meadow and finally into grassland as the procession wended its way into a lush river valley. The grassland turned into cultivated fields thick with green, waist-high corn plants. There was a lot of activity in the fields. The workers stopped to greet the procession, calling out to the warriors, who answered with glad cries and waves of their own. Except Gray Hair. He stalked on with unheeding dignity.

The workers' greetings soon turned into gasps of astonishment when they spotted SStragh. A crowd gathered to stare at the lizard. They were clearly amazed, but not so shocked that they ran screaming with fright. SStragh strode ahead with the same aplomb as Gray Hair, not deigning to notice the people.

A palisade-enclosed village lay beyond the fields. The palisade was made of sharp-pointed logs ten feet high set in front of earth walls. Inside the village, towering above the stockade, were nearly a dozen little hills. These earthen hills were flat-topped and had rectangular buildings on their crests.

The palisade's double-doored gate was open. A stream of men, women, children, and dogs came running from the village to greet the warriors and stare at the newcomers. There were a lot of people, easily several hundred.

Eckels had a sudden queasy feeling as they entered the village. Maybe, he thought, looking at the high walls, the gate manned by tattooed warriors armed with bows and arrows, spears, and the occasional antique-looking rifle, maybe it wouldn't be so easy to escape from this place after all.

Maybe he was stuck here. Really and truly stuck, forever and for all time. If that was the case, he thought, carefully watching the stoic Gray Hair as he led the procession through the welcoming throng, he'd better find the headman's good side, and get on it. Fast.

He watched the hobbled prisoners stumble through the village. Half of the crowd was staring at SStragh, the other half was jeering at the prisoners. A few were throwing clods of dirt at them.

Eckels had no idea what their ultimate fate would be, but something told him that it wouldn't be very pleasant. Whatever it was, he had no desire to share it with them. None at all.

9

Bad News

Aaron walked down the garden path, stopping to watch the tableau by the lushly planted fish pond at the end of the trail.

The setting sun reflected redly off the pond's rippling surface as Jennifer fed crumbs of food to the pond's inhabitants. Gigantic carp, colored white, black, gold, and red, roiled at the surface, so eager for the bits of food that they were a solid mass of flashing colors glittering like sparkling fireworks in the sunset.

Jennifer was wearing a white kimono tied with a blue sash. Her golden brown hair fell to her shoulders, flashing in the sunlight like the colorful fish she was feeding.

Two of the household maids were with her. They were all laughing at the fish, who were so eager for food that they almost took it from their hands. No one seemed to notice the samurai guard, who stood unobtrusively near the pond in the shade of the willow trees whose branches trailed so low that their tips dipped into the water.

Aaron cleared his throat. Jennifer and the maids looked up with the happy, laughing expressions of children at play. Jennifer rose gracefully to her feet and came to Aaron. They embraced, hugging each other fiercely. The maids moved away discreetly, crossing the little arched bridge that led to the other side of the pond. The fish followed them, hoping for more food. The samurai kept his place.

"Did you see the koi, Aaron?" Jennifer asked. "Weren't they beautiful?"

"Sure," Aaron said. "For fish. But I'm more worried about you. Are they treating you all right? Have you had anything to eat? Are—"

"Slow down," Jennifer said, laughing. "I'm fine. They've taken wonderful care of me. I've had a nice, heavenly bath, and plenty to eat. SStragh and some of the other Mutata treated me well, but it's great to be among human beings again. It's especially great to be with you."

"I'll say."

They sat down on the backless wooden bench that looked out over the fish pond. Aaron put his arm around Jennifer's shoulders and she snuggled comfortably into place.

"I came as soon as I got your note," Aaron said. "You said that you had something to tell me?"

For a while Jennifer said nothing. She watched as the maids studiously fed the fish and didn't watch them. Finally she sighed and said, "I'm afraid that I've got some bad news."

Aaron squeezed her shoulder and smiled down at her. "Hey, how bad could it be? We're together again."

Jennifer looked back up at him, her blue eyes serious and sad. "I'm afraid it's pretty bad. I wanted to tell you sooner, but there just wasn't any time. At first I was so happy to be with you, then we were separated again. It's—it's about Grandpa Carl."

Aaron frowned. "What about him?"

"I—Aaron, there's no good way to tell you this. I found him near Eckels's cave in the Mutata valley. He'd been killed by a Gairk."

"Grandpa Carl?" Aaron asked. He felt all his happiness, all his strength ooze out of him like air from a punctured balloon. "Dead?"

Jennifer only nodded.

"He . . . he must have come for me . . . He must have come looking for me."

Aaron blinked away sudden tears. One escaped, dropping from his eyelash, and ran down his right cheek. He felt cold and empty at the same time, and then was overwhelmed by memories of his grandfather and the times they'd had together. Grandpa Carl had played ball with him when he was young. Taught him how to fish. How to drive a car. They were close, close as the brother Aaron had never had, bound together in the love that only a boy and his father's father could have. Grandpa Carl was gone. And it was his fault . . .

He hunched over as the tears broke free. He couldn't stop them. Jennifer cradled him in her arms and spoke to him as he cried. He couldn't understand her words, only the soothing sound of her voice murmuring to him, the warmth of her arms holding him.

After awhile he caught his breath with a shudder and sat up, wiping at his eyes with the palms of his hands. The maids were nowhere to be seen. The samurai guard looked ahead, stoic and unseeing.

"It's my fault," Aaron said. "It's my fault that he's dead."

Jennifer shook her head. "No one is to blame. Is it your fault that he loved you enough to try to help you?"

Aaron blinked, wiping away his last tears. He couldn't think now. Maybe Jennifer was right. Maybe it wasn't his fault; maybe it was. Ultimately, though, his grandfather's death had been caused by the unraveling of the timestream.

Somehow, some way, Aaron vowed that he would put it all back together. He wouldn't just find their home. Somehow, some way, he would fix everything. It would be his monument to the memory of his grandfather. It would be his penance for the guilt he felt about his grandfather's death.

"We've got to fix things," he said, looking out over the beautiful garden now settling down to darkness as the sun slipped over the horizon. "We've got to make things right. You and me and Travis. Your friend SStragh. Even Peter. Even Mundo, We've got to set things right for everyone."

"We will," Jennifer said quietly. "We will."

Peter was bored.

Travis was off somewhere with Captain Otomo, drinking sake out of tiny porcelain cups. They didn't talk each other's language, but somehow they recognized that they were alike and an instinctive bond had developed between them.

That's just fine, Peter told himself, but he wasn't part of their club. He didn't want to be. Right now they were probably drinking, showing each other their weapons, and mumbling incomprehensibly at each other. Let them. Besides, Peter didn't like the taste of sake.

He didn't feel like hanging out with Mundo, either, but he couldn't even if he wanted to. Lord Akira

Yoshinori had summoned the talking monkey some time ago and the ape had disappeared into the inner recesses of the citadel. They were probably off together plotting something, but exactly what Peter couldn't even begin to imagine.

That left Jennifer, but Peter had no idea where she was. He hadn't really had a chance to talk with her since they had linked up again. He had the feeling—well, it was more than a feeling—that she wasn't very happy with the way he'd acted when they'd been captives of the Mutata. Then, of course, he had made the break with Eckels and she'd got left behind. But that wasn't his fault. It was just the way things had worked out.

Maybe if he could find her, he could explain things to her. Of course, Aaron was back on the scene. That would make things tougher. But Peter still hoped that someday he would make Jennifer see that he was the right one for her, not Aaron.

But first he had to find her.

The Japanese let him wander alone around the citadel without a guard. He was only one man, he was unarmed, and they knew as well as he did that he wasn't going to go anywhere. He knew better than to try to crash Lord Akira's inner sanctuary, which was the only part of the citadel guarded by sentries. They looked at him suspiciously as he passed by their station, but made no move to intercept him.

"Hi, fellows," Peter said cheerily. "Lord High Muckamuck still in confab with the monkey?"

The sentries exchanged baffled glances.

"Never mind. Say, you know where I can find that kid Katsu? He'd be able to guide me around." Peter made a face of disgust when the sentries didn't respond. "Katsu. You know, Katsu?"

One of them finally nodded.

"Ahh, Katsu." He let loose a quick stream of words, none of which Peter understood.

"You'll have to do better than that," Peter said.

The two guards exchanged glances, then one of them looked at Peter. He held his hands out in front of him close together and made a strange rocking motion. He threw back his head and made a whinnying sound.

Peter frowned, then nodded. "I get it. Horses." He made the whinnying sound himself and the guards nodded eagerly and smiled. "Katsu is with the horses. Okay. You guys are great at charades."

Now, Peter said to himself as he walked off, *if I can only find the stables.*

He'd noticed a corral in the village before they'd entered the citadel. Peter didn't know if they would let him wander around the village alone, but decided to cross that bridge when he came to it.

And he did. The guards at the bridge across the citadel's moat didn't even blink an eye when Peter strolled past them and went down into the village. Peter gave them a cheery wave as he went by.

"Just going to get some fresh air," he said breezily.

Actually, the air did smell fresh. Devoid of any taint of petrochemical contamination, it smelled great until Peter got close to the stables. There it reeked with a much older form of pollution.

"Phew!" Peter muttered to himself. "And people say that car exhaust smells bad!"

Peter figured that Katsu, lowly servant that he was, was mucking out a stall somewhere. He didn't fell like entering the actual stables, where the manure odor would only be intensified, so he stood outside the door and called, "Katsu! Come here, will you? Katsu!"

There was no answer. Peter sighed deeply and entered the building.

"Katsu! It's Peter! You here?"

It was dark inside and the smell was worse than he'd imagined. Breathing through his mouth, he called "If you're here, come on out already. Is that you, Katsu?"

A small figure moved through the darkness. Peter followed him, getting more annoyed by the second. He reached out, grabbed him by the shoulder and turned him around.

"What's the matter with you?" he asked. "You deaf, Katsu?"

Only it wasn't Katsu. Katsu didn't have fangs that gleamed in the dim light, or a hairy face, or strong, leathery hands that effortlessly broke Peter's grip. Startled, Peter jumped backward until he realized who it was.

"Mundo! You really scared me! Say, what are you doing out here, anyway? Are you trying to escape?"

"You ask a lot of questions that are none of your business," Mundo said loftily.

"Maybe not," Peter blustered. "We're all in this together. If you do something foolish—"

Movement in the stall behind him made Peter turn. There were two more cloaked figures that he could barely discern in the light cast by the paper-walled lantern that one of them held. The one with the lantern was an Indian. He was dressed differently than the ones Peter had seen so far, wearing a short kiltlike skirt and not much else. His face and body were tattooed all over with bluish blotches and lines and geometric figures. He wore an ornament, a white pendant the size and shape of a small dish, around his neck. It shone brightly in the light cast by the lantern, looking like a small, featureless moon.

The second man was Japanese. Peter stared at him for a second before it registered on Peter's surprised brain who the man was.

"Lord Akira," he said. "What are you doing here?"

He looked at Mundo, the only one able to answer him.

Akira said something clipped and harsh in Japanese. Mundo answered him while looking intently at Peter.

"What's going on?" Peter asked. "What did he say?"

"Lord Akira said that it was unfortunate that you came snooping around here. It was most unfortunate that you recognized him."

"I was only looking for Katsu," Peter said quickly, realizing suddenly that for some reason he was in big trouble. "I can see he's not here. I'll be going now."

Akira spat out a few more words in Japanese. Mundo smiled, exposing his long, glittering fangs.

"I'm afraid that's not possible."

He grabbed Peter's arm. Peter tried to shake him off, but the ape was a lot stronger. He opened his mouth to shout for help, but Mundo quickly clamped a large, hairy hand over his lips. He tried to bite, but his teeth couldn't get a purchase on Mundo's leathery palm. He kicked out and had the satisfaction of landing a solid blow on Mundo's shin. Mundo winced, but held on.

Peter drew his foot back to kick again, then something hard crashed on the back of his head. He tried to shake off the effects of the blow, but couldn't. His knees went rubbery as he lost the strength in his legs and slumped to the stable floor, unconscious.

10

Rendezvous in the Night

SStragh was starting to appreciate how Jhenini must have felt when she'd been marooned alone among an alien race.

So far the humans had not treated her unkindly, or even threatened her in any way. They had even let her keep her spear. That was what had made SStragh decide to go along with them. So far they were treating her as something between a welcome guest and a respected captive. Making allowances for their alien customs, that wasn't so bad. True, they had prevented her from finishing her confrontation with Eikels, but she was patient. She could wait.

The people at the human village were astonished to see her. She ignored them as best she could, though SStragh saw plenty to marvel at herself. The alien sights, sounds, and smells threatened to overload her senses and she realized for the first time how brave Jhenini had been. Jhenini had not given in to the strangeness of everything when she'd been captured by the Mutata. SStragh resolved to be as brave as the female human.

The procession stopped in the middle of the village where the human in charge of the group who had captured them gave a long speech to the assembled crowd.

SStragh listened hard, but could understand none of it. The sounds he made were similar to those Jhenini made, but they seemed to be arranged in totally different patterns and spoken in a totally different rhythm. She had picked up a few words of Jhenini's language during their weeks of close interaction, but she could understand nothing of this speech whatsoever.

The group broke up after the human finished his speech. The chained humans were led away. Eikels went off with the human in charge. Other humans gestured for SStragh to follow them. She did, without protest.

This village was very different from the Mutata village where SStragh lived on the dinosaur world. The dwellings didn't connect to each other as they did in SStragh's village. They were rectangular, with sharply angled walls and ceilings where the Mutata's buildings had soft angles that flowed in smooth curves.

The buildings in the human village were arranged in patterns. Some, like those to which they led Eikels, were on the tops or sides of the flat hills that were scattered around the enclosure. Others, like the one SStragh was taken to, were on the ground. These buildings were clustered in little groups and arranged so that they faced the big open space in the middle of the village. It seemed that the humans did many of their daily tasks in this open space.

They were tending fires, scraping hides, preparing food, and chipping rocks to make finely formed stone tools. They still watched SStragh as she passed, but her presence was not enough to keep them from their chores.

SStragh was taken into one of the rectangular buildings. It was empty, but the human smell clung closely to it. She had to stoop to enter through the building's small doorway, but once inside she was able to stand up comfortably.

The warriors who led her to the building then went away. When SStragh peered out through the hide-covered doorway she saw that two had remained behind as a guard. So they didn't trust her entirely. Still, neither did they insult her by trying to take her spear away. That was good.

She set the spear aside and tried to make herself comfortable on the dirt floor. It was not *too* uncomfortable, but neither were there worn couches and soft leaning pads like those in her snug little compartment back in the Mutata village. Her discomfort was increased by the fact that she was starting to feel hunger pangs. She hadn't eaten all day, except for a few sour-tasting leaves.

Just as her stomach rumbled aloud in angry protest at its emptiness, the door's hide cover was pushed aside and a female human entered the building. SStragh could smell the fear that inundated this one, so she remained still in what she hoped was a nonthreatening posture.

The human female came in quickly and put a platter down on the ground before SStragh. It had food on it. SStragh grumbled a polite thank you and the female turned and ran. The two guards poked their heads into the room, but exchanged shrugs when they saw SStragh sitting peacefully on the floor. They returned to their posts.

SStragh leaned over the food, sniffing it cautiously. Her lips curled in sudden distaste as she caught a whiff of dead, burned meat. Her stomachs flip-flopped and for a moment indignation threatened to overcome the equanimity with which she had so far faced this strange world.

Did they think she was a predator, an eater of dead flesh, to offer her such food?

For a moment her mind burned with the insult, then rationality returned. They could not know that the Mutata ate only plants. That realization caused SStragh to sit back on her haunches and think.

What insults, she wondered, had the Mutata so casually handed to Jhenini during her captivity at their village? The paths taken by the Mutata and the humans were so different, so much more divergent than SStragh would ever have guessed.

SStragh moved the dish of cooked meat away from the platter of food, taking it to the far corner of the room, so that its smell wouldn't contaminate the other food that the humans had offered her. That done, she found things much more palatable than burned animal flesh.

There was a succulent vegetable that had been boiled until it was soft and cakes made of ground flour of a different sort of vegetable. SStragh found both of these dishes quite palatable, but lacking in sufficient quantity to soothe the hunger pangs raging in her belly.

Nevertheless it was good, edible food. It would keep her nourished. She could survive on this world.

Once she had eaten, there was nothing for SStragh to do but stand around and think. She didn't worry about herself personally. Her kind did not have a strong sense of self-interest. The Mutata thought more in terms of group instead of personal survival. But her experiences so far had given her a lot to meditate on concerning the OColihi, convincing her that it must be changed.

It got cooler as night fell, but SStragh simply passed the hours in a deep state of meditation-rest that served the Mutata as sleep.

Late in the night, though, SStragh's finely honed senses brought her to instant alertness as she realized that a party of humans were about to enter her enclosure.

There were three humans in the group as well as one who looked somewhat human and smelled somewhat human, but wasn't quite right. He was shorter and much hairier and wore none of the coverings that the humans liked to drape themselves with. He had an acrid animal scent to him, but he did walk on two legs like the other humans and conversed with them in both their languages. In fact, he seemed to be translating between the tribesmen who had captured SStragh and Eikels, and the other man, who seemed to be of the warrior tribe whose members occasionally appeared in SStragh's home valley in the dinosaur world.

This newcomer was very excited to see SStragh. He couldn't take his eyes off her. SStragh got the feeling that they were discussing her fate, that they were haggling over her. It was not a pleasant feeling to have. SStragh felt a stab of guilt as she realized that this must have been how Jhenini had felt when the Mutata had been squabbling about her and Peeitah.

Finally, SStragh could take no more.

"I am present," she said with hurt dignity, altering her scent to allow a hint of tart annoyance to creep in. "If you wish to discuss my fate, you should discuss it with me."

Of course, SStragh realized that this was a hopeless request, because no one on this entire world but she and Jhenini spoke the Mutata language.

Her surprise was great when the little almost-human turned to her and smiled an almost-human smile, exposing fanged teeth more suitable for a miniature Gairk.

"Very well," he said in passable Mutata, "we shall."

Mundo thought that Lord Akira would fall over in astonishment when he realized that he and the reptilian creature were actually conversing.

"You can really talk with it?" Akira asked in utter astonishment.

Mundo nodded casually. "Of course. It is well within my powers to converse with any being in this world."

"How remarkable. You are truly the Monkey King," Akira said. "And it is a great omen that you've come to me."

Mundo smiled to himself. Akira was a foolish man, easily led. Mundo had limited mind-reading ability—he was a skimmer, able to discern someone's surface thoughts if she wasn't on guard against such an intrusion—but Akira was like an open book. The hints Mundo got from his surface thoughts plus Mundo's increasing ability to read human expressions and emotions made it easy to delve into Akira's innermost being. And what he'd found there was surprising.

The Japanese lord hated his post on the edge of nowhere. For some time he had been having secret talks with the Hill Makers, who were his greatest enemies. Mundo's resemblance to the Monkey King had enabled him quickly to take things in hand—or paw—and exert immediate control over Akira by subtly encouraging him to act on a plan that Akira had been tiptoeing around for some months.

Mundo's motivations were of the highest sort. Of course, Mundo's primary motivations were taking care of himself first, last, and foremost. He hoped to worm his way into Akira's favor and be given complete control over the time machine that Eckels had brought into this world. Given enough of an opportunity he was sure that he could figure out its complexities—after all, both Aaron and Travis, inferior beings that they were, had no difficulties with it. Even if for some inexplicable reason he couldn't figure out how to work the thing, as Akira's favorite he would surely be in a position to exert certain pressures on Aaron or Travis to make them take him back to his home timeline.

But to become Akira's favorite he had to give the lord what he wanted. Unused to the human mind, Mundo couldn't understand why Akira was fixated on the notion of dragons. But the lord was and Mundo could certainly get him one. When word had come from Akira's contacts in the Hill Maker camp that they had captured a dragon, it had taken little effort on Mundo's part to convince Akira that they should see it that very night.

Of course, they had to go to the meeting secretly. It wouldn't do to let it be known that Lord Akira was consorting with the Nipponjins' deadliest enemies. For a moment things had teetered precariously when that blockhead Peter had shown up at the stables. But they'd taken care of him easily enough. Then it was only a matter of bundling up Akira so that he wouldn't be recognized, showing a signed pass at the gate, and they were out into the night.

"It is as I told you, Lord Akira," Mundo said ingratiatingly, "trust in me and you shall have all you desire. Did I not tell you that a dragon would be yours if you listened to me?"

"Indeed you did," Akira said. He turned to look at the Hill Makers' chief, but continued to speak to Mundo. "Ask them what they want for the creature."

"Certainly," Mundo said in Japanese. He then turned to the chief of the Hill Makers and spoke perfectly in their tongue. "My Lord Akira is very much interested in acquiring this creature for his own personal, um, use." Though what that would be Mundo couldn't imagine. "It is, well, a somewhat scrawny specimen, not as magnificent and resplendent as those fabled in song and legend, but, being the only one found in these parts, would certainly do. My Lord Akira instructs me to ask what sort of commodity you would expect in exchange for this creature."

The chief, named Gray Raven because of the streaks in his otherwise midnight black hair, was in his middle years, but he was still an impressive physical specimen. He also possessed a rather devious and subtle mind. Mundo knew that the chief was planning something, exactly what he couldn't yet discern.

"Well," Gray Raven said slowly, "as you said, this is a unique creature. We have never seen one before, except occasionally in brief glimpses during the storms that have ravaged our valley lately. We have no use for it. If your chief desires it, he may have it as a gift from me to him."

"It's certainly a unique and handsome gift," Mundo said. "I'm sure Lord Akira would like me to offer you something in return. Do you have any suggestions?"

Gray Raven smiled. "Peace," he said. "Peace between our people."

"A worthy goal," Mundo said. "Do you have any ideas how this could be achieved?"

"Yes," Gray Raven replied. "Yes, I do."

11

Missing

The morning came quickly for Aaron. It had been a strange night. He'd been dead tired, but the news of Grandpa Carl's death combined with the excitement of being in a strange place and the elation of finding Jennifer had made sleep difficult.

The citadel room set aside for himself, Travis, and Peter was also an odd mixture of comfort and discomfort. There were no beds, just quilts on top of the tatami mats that were the universal floor covering in the citadel. The quilt-tatami combination proved quite comfortable. The same could not be said for the Japanese version of a pillow, which was a small wooden platform with a curved surface that fitted the back of the sleeper's head.

Using one, Aaron soon found, was like trying to sleep with your head on a curved rock. After the beginning of a bad sore neck, Aaron abandoned the chopping block and fell asleep with his head pillowed on his arm.

He awoke with the first rays of sunlight filtering through the unshuttered windows, more refreshed and relaxed than he had been for the past few days. He sat up, rubbed his eyes, and looked over at Travis, who was sleeping on a tatami to Aaron's right. The loss he felt for Grandpa Carl was still present. It would be for a long time.

"Come on, Travis," Aaron said loudly. "Time's wasting. The sun's up and we should be out hunting the time machine."

Travis opened one eye and peered at Aaron. He groaned and rolled over, turning away from his companion.

"Come on," Aaron said. "You don't want Eckels to get away, do you?"

The name of his foe worked its usual magic on Travis. The hunter sat up and groaned more loudly. He looked at Aaron through bloodshot eyes. His expression was that of a sick dog.

"Too much sake last night?" Aaron asked.

Travis cleared his throat experimentally, then shook his head, which he immediately regretted.

"Too much," he croaked in agreement. "But I'd like to see the other guy right now."

"Captain Otomo?"

Travis started to nod, then thought better of it.

"Right. You know, he's not such a bad guy when you get to know him. 'Course, if we spoke each other's language, then maybe I'd get to know him even better and wouldn't think he was such a great guy. Who knows?" Travis rose creakily to his feet. "I think I'll go shave my tongue. Say." He stopped, frowned, and pointed past Aaron. "Peter must be an early riser."

Aaron turned and for the first time looked at the tatami mat to his left, which had been reserved for Peter. It was empty.

Aaron frowned himself. "I don't think that mat's been slept on," he said.

Travis vigorously rubbed his lean, stubbly bearded face. "Nah. The kid probably got up and made his bed before he left."

"Without waking us up?" Aaron asked skeptically. "And if you think Peter would make his own bed . . . well, you just don't know Peter."

"Then where is he?" Travis asked.

Aaron shrugged. "That's the question."

He got up and went to the sleeping chamber's only door. He slid it open quietly on its well-oiled track, but still woke Katsu, who was sleeping in the hallway right in front of the door.

Katsu looked up, knuckling the sleep from his eyes. He got to his knees, bowing before Aaron.

"*Hai*," he said, in a questioning manner.

"Great," Aaron muttered. Where was Mundo when you really needed him? *Maybe*, he thought, *off with Peter*? Aaron took a deep breath. "Katsu," he said, to gain the servant's attention. He had to repeat the name before the boy looked up at him. *Now what*? he asked himself. He thought about it for a moment, then pointed into the sleeping chamber. "Peter?" he asked, exaggerating the questioning tone in his voice and pointing at the unused quilt and tatami.

Katsu looked at him, looked where he was pointing, then looked back.

"Peter?" Aaron asked, again exaggerating the questioning tone and this time adding a little pantomime as if he were looking for something.

Katsu frowned and then suddenly nodded. "Ah, Peter-san," he said, then he launched into a long speech apparently explaining that he didn't know where Peter was because he ended it with a shrug and a baffled expression on his own face.

"That's terrific," Aaron said. He stuck his head back into the room and said to Travis, "Peter's missing. I think Katsu thought he was with us. But I can't be sure."

"Well, see if he knows where Mundo is. Maybe *he* can explain things."

"Good idea." Aaron turned back to Katsu and with the same exaggerated voice and pantomime said "Mundo?"

"Hai," Katsu said, nodding vigorously. *"Daimyo Akira."*

He added hand motions apparently signifying that the two were together. Travis poked his head out of the room in time to catch the last of Katsu's mimed explanation.

"Well, that's just great," Aaron said. "Apparently Mundo is off with that big shot Akira. What do you suppose he sees in him, anyway?"

"The monkey or the big shot?" Travis asked. "Never mind that. There's always Jennifer. *If* we can track her down, maybe she can explain things."

Aaron looked hopefully at Katsu. "Jennifer?"

Katsu nodded. *"Hai."*

"Jennifer," Aaron repeated. He pointed down to the floor right at their feet. "Jennifer. Here." He pointed again for emphasis.

Katsu seemed to understand. He bowed deeply several times, exclaimed *"Hai,"* and then went off down the corridor.

"Well," Travis said, "maybe we're finally getting somewhere."

"We'd better be," Aaron said darkly. He didn't want to add that he'd just found Jennifer and he didn't want to lose her again so soon. He didn't have to say it, though. Travis could read his emotions in the way he stared down the corridor after Katsu, half-eager to see Jennifer again, half-worried that she'd be missing like Peter and Mundo.

Aaron needn't have worried. Jennifer arrived shortly, Katsu trailing a couple of respectful paces behind her. Aaron filled her in and Jennifer questioned Katsu but learned nothing new. When he'd bedded down for the night, Katsu had thought Peter was in the sleeping chamber with Aaron and Travis. He had no idea where Peter could be. As for Mundo, he was with Lord Akira, who had apparently taken quite a shine to him.

"I don't know if I like that," Aaron said. "Mundo has yet to prove that he can be trusted."

Jennifer shrugged. "What harm could he cause?"

"I don't know," Aaron said darkly. "He has a devious mind. And it's usually stuck thinking about himself."

"I know one thing," Jennifer said. "If we're to get anything done, I have to get out of these clothes."

She held her arms out to illustrate her point. The silken kimono she had on was beautiful, with a rich, lush fabric, wonderfully subtle coloring, and exquisite embroidering, but it was not a practical garment. The sleeves were long, wide, and heavy. The skirt part of it was long enough to drag on the floor and bulky enough to make quick movements impossible.

"The only thing is," Jennifer said, "my clothes were so filthy and worn that they got thrown away." She turned to Katsu and addressed him in Japanese. "I'll need men's clothing," she told him. "Nothing elaborate, just trousers and a top."

Katsu looked at her with wide eyes. "I–I don't know, Jennifer-san."

"I do," she said in a tone that brooked no argument.

Katsu bowed and scurried off to find suitable clothing.

"What are we going to do about Peter?" Jennifer asked.

Aaron shook his head. "We've got to try to find him. Who knows what trouble he could get into—or has already."

"If Mundo is really in as good with Lord Akira as Katsu says," Travis suggested, "he could help us get to the bottom of things."

"If he wants to," Aaron said doubtfully.

Katsu arrived momentarily with the clothing that Jennifer had requested. She went into the bedchamber to change and came back out looking like the star in one of those improbable movies where a woman tries to disguise herself by dressing in men's clothing. Katsu looked doubtful, but Jennifer felt really free for the first time since their arrival in this timeline. The clothing she'd been wearing up until now had been very beautiful, but it had also been very confining to her free and active spirit.

"Ask Katsu if we can see Lord Akira," Aaron suggested.

"All right," Jennifer said, "but I don't think that will be very easy, unless for some reason he wants to see us."

Katsu, again, confirmed Jennifer's suspicions. Lord Akira had very little to do with the ordinary people of his holding. Jennifer, Aaron, and Travis had a certain amount of status as guests, but they were suspicious characters at best, with no real formal standing in this world. They could put in a request to see Akira to the majordomo. He was the official who ran the day-to-day operations of the citadel. Since one of his main duties was keeping Akira from being annoyed by people who wanted to see him, Katsu doubted that they'd be granted an audience.

"There's always Captain Otomo," Travis said. "He probably knows more about what's going on around here than Akira anyway."

"All right," Jennifer said. "Take us to him."

Otomo was surprised, but not displeased, to see them. Showing no ill effects from the immense amount of sake he had quaffed with Travis the night before, he was having his morning rice. He invited them all to join. Except Katsu, of course. The servant boy knelt unobtrusively in the rear of the chamber while Otomo and his guests ate a spartan meal of rice, pickled vegetables, dried fish, and hot tea.

Aaron found the food simple, but a bit more to his taste than the fancier dishes that had been served the night before. A servant cleared the dishes away while they lingered over a final cup of tea. Aaron wondered how best to broach the subject of Peter's disappearance, then decided that the only way was to come right out and question Otomo directly.

Otomo frowned when Jennifer questioned him. If he was disturbed by her unconventional clothing, he didn't show it. As was the case in their native timeline, Aaron realized that this society took politeness to an extreme. Otomo listened carefully to Jennifer's questions. His reply was short, accompanied by a quick shake of the head that neither Aaron nor Travis needed translated.

"He doesn't know anything about Peter, does he?" Aaron asked.

Jennifer shook her head. "No, but he's going to look into it."

"Katsu," Otomo called out gruffly, and the servant boy bowed his forehead to the floor. Otomo rattled off a string of orders, Katsu exclaimed *"Hai,"* once or twice, then sprang up and quickly left the chamber.

"Captain Otomo," Jennifer explained, "has told Katsu to question the men who were on guard duty last night. He said to bring any who saw Peter. He also requested that Katsu bring one of the samurai who'd been guarding the outer gate so we can make sure that Peter didn't leave the village last night."

"Thank you," Aaron told him with a small bow. *"Arigato."*

Otomo gave a gruff grunt accompanied by his usual millimeter-deep bow.

"Ask him," Travis said, "if it'll be all right if we go looking for Eckels today."

Jennifer relayed the question, then Otomo's reply.

"He says certainly, but you must realize it's dangerous outside the village walls. Hill Makers are in the vicinity and Iroquois war parties have been spotted nearby as well. He offers the use of his Indian trackers, as well as a squad of soldiers. I think," Jennifer added, "that it would be a good idea to take him up on this."

"We don't need the trackers," Travis said. "I've been trailing all kinds of creatures all my life."

"But taking along a squad of soldiers would be smart," Aaron said.

Travis nodded. "Amen to that."

As Jennifer thanked Otomo, Katsu returned with three samurai. They bowed before Otomo with the serious regard for ceremony that the Nipponjin always showed. Otomo questioned them one at a time and they told what they knew without any prodding on Otomo's part.

The first samurai had been one of the guards posted at Lord Akira's chamber. He related how he and a companion saw Peter-san wandering through the halls looking for the serving boy Katsu. At least they assumed that's what he was doing. The language barrier prevented them from being more precise. At any rate, one of the guards finally got across the point that Katsu was doing chores in the stable and Peter-san went off, presumably to the stable. That was the last they saw of him.

The second samurai had been guarding the footbridge leading across the citadel's moat to the village.

He confirmed that Peter-san had passed his post shortly after the other samurai had sent him to the stable. He had seemed cheerful enough, and was alone.

"And," Otomo asked Katsu (as Jennifer translated), "Peter-san never found you?"

The boy shook his head. "I saw no one. I'd finished with the horses early and left the stables shortly after sunset."

When Otomo questioned the third samurai he discovered that early in the evening there hadn't been much traffic in or out of the village. The only notable exception was a cloaked messenger to Lord Akira. He was an Indian, but he had borne Akira's personal seal and therefore was beyond reproach or question.

"Nothing else happened of note?" Otomo asked.

"Well," the samurai replied, "not until the messenger left, of course. He was accompanied by two others who also wore cloaks, but neither could have been Peter-san. I'd seen him when he'd first come to the village and he's much larger than any of the cloaked figures who went out through the gate."

"It sounds as if you spent a very quiet night," Otomo said.

"Yes, sir," the samurai replied. "At least until close to dawn when Lord Akira came back."

"Lord Akira came back?" Otomo repeated. Everyone could see that he was plainly astonished. "Then, he was one of the cloaked figures who'd gone out earlier?"

"He must have been," the samurai said. "I never made the connection until now. It must have been all the excitement."

"Excitement? What excitement?"

It was the samurai's turn to be astonished. "Didn't you know? I thought everyone had heard."

"Heard what?"

Aaron and Travis didn't need the benefit of Jennifer's translation to see that Otomo's astonishment had turned to annoyance bordering on anger.

"Why, last night Lord Akira found a dragon in the forest. He brought it back with him. Everyone is talking about it."

"A dragon?" Otomo shouted. "What nonsense is this?"

"A dragon?" Aaron repeated as Jennifer translated the conversation into English.

Jennifer looked worried.

"It must be SStragh," she said.

12

Morning on the Hill

The hut was a step up from the cave, Eckels thought, but just barely.

The food was decent. At least he didn't have to catch it, kill it, skin it, and cook it himself. The vegetables were nice, too.

He'd fallen asleep thinking that if he couldn't find his way home, this wouldn't be a bad world to be marooned in. The people were savages, of course, but at least they were people and not lizards. He could handle people. He could always handle people. It was what he did best.

He fell asleep to visions of what he could do with his superior knowledge and intellect in a world like this. He dreamed that he slowly but surely built an expanding power base until he dominated the entire region. He dreamed that he showed these people what it was like to have a king. He dreamed that he turned this savage world into a very pleasant place. At least for himself.

His sleep was finally broken by a weird, persistent tolling sound. It was like nothing he'd ever heard before, but sounded something like a bassoon or small tuba blowing down from some great height.

He crawled out from the warm heap of finely made fur blankets that was his bed and groggily wiped at his face. The summons persisted, rising and falling like the baying of a great beast over the sleeping Hill Maker village.

It was, Eckels realized, a call to wakefulness. Maybe, he thought, it was an alarm of some kind. Maybe the village was under attack. He quickly threw on his clothes, carefully stuck his unsheathed sword through his belt, and stumbled out of the small hut he had been given at the base of one of the tall mounds that dominated the interior of the village.

It was just past dawn. The rising sun had not yet warmed the air or taken the dew from the grass. A slight fog hung on the chill air, lending a hint of mystery to the scene.

None of the villagers seemed alarmed by the strange summons, though they all were drawn to the spot where it originated. Eckels fell in with the villagers who, when they took notice of him at all, murmured what he supposed were polite greetings and simply continued on their way.

The villagers were converging on the largest of the man-made mounds. This earth pyramid was on the south side of the village, abutting the protective palisade. Rising more than a hundred feet into the air, it was really a series of mounds piled atop each other in four steps. Each flat-topped hillock formed the foundation for the succeeding mounds and also had several rectangular huts on it.

The lowest level had five structures crowded upon it. The sound was coming from there. Five men dressed in kilts and feather headdresses were blowing into large seashells, producing the bellowing, booming notes that rolled across the silent village below.

As Eckels came closer he could see that these men were tattooed all over their faces, limbs, and bodies and all wore the white moonlike pendant. They paid no attention to the people converging at the base of the mound, but continued to blow their shell horns with all their might.

The villagers stopped at the foot of the broad earthen ramp that ran up the side of the pyramid to the base of the upper level. The crowd waited patiently as the men continued their droning call until everyone in the village was gathered at the base of the ramp.

Then the horns stopped. The village became silent again. There was no talking, no whispering in the ranks of the assembled villagers. Eckels waited patiently, if a bit bewilderedly, to see what would happen next.

The men put aside their shells and silently trudged up the ramp until they reached the top level of the pyramid and entered one of the two rectangular huts on that level. They each came out dragging a bound prisoner.

As the prisoners appeared the villagers surged forward, slowly climbing the earth ramp to the pyramid's top. Eckels moved with them, subtly pushing forward to reach the front. He wanted a good view of whatever was going to happen.

Once the people had climbed as high as they could without actually stepping on the uppermost pyramid, an air of silent, unmoving expectancy came upon the crowd.

Eckels got a good view of the prisoners and their captors, as well as the structures on the pyramid. What he saw didn't bode well for the captives silently awaiting their fate.

The huts were long and rectangular, like the one he had spent the night in, like the ones that were the dwellings of the common villagers. Basically they were built of the same materials and had the same thatch and pole construction. They were no bigger, nor better made.

The only difference was the sinister decorations hung upon the huts' roofs and eaves. Life-size bird effigies carved out of wood and decorated with feathers looked like waiting vultures perched upon the roof. Skulls, animal and human both, sat in long rows upon the eaves, staring down in mute disapproval.

"Poor jerks," Eckels said aloud as he, along with the rest of the village, stood patiently waiting in the cool dawn air.

A figure suddenly appeared through the doorway of the second hut on the top of the pyramid. Eckels couldn't be sure, but he thought it was the chief he called Gray Hair.

An intricate bird-mask hid the man's face and a cloak of feathers hung upon his arms as if they were wings. The feathers were mottled gray, brown, and dirty white. The huge-beaked mask gave Gray Hair the features of a vulture.

Gray Hair stood in front of a flat-topped altar set up equidistant between the two huts. One of the priests, as Eckels suddenly realized these men were, dragged his captive, one of the badly wounded samurai, over to the altar. The prisoner was either drugged or hopeless. He offered no resistance as he was laid upon the altar and bound securely to it. Gray Hair lifted his arms wide, his feathered cloak spreading out like great wings, and began to speak.

His words seemed to address neither the captive nor the crowd that was raptly watching his every action. It looked as if he were speaking to the sky, or perhaps the dawning sun, still a swollen red ball hanging low upon the horizon.

Gray Hair's speech reached an abrupt, unexpected crescendo and his arms suddenly plunged downward. Eckels realized that he was holding a long knife chipped from some kind of dark stone. He plunged the knife into the captive's abdomen and slashed upward. If the man screamed, the sound was hidden by the sudden collective release of breath by the watching villagers. The captive strained upward against his bonds for a brief moment, then fell back in the complete laxity of death.

Gray Hair made another cut, totally opening up his victim's abdomen. He laid aside the knife and leaned over the body, peering intently at the gory wound. He uttered a loud cry and plunged a hand into the samurai's body and pulled something out. He held it up to the crowd and shouted triumphantly.

Eckels looked away, feeling vaguely ill. Even his extensive hunting experience hadn't prepared him for something like this.

"Pretty disgusting, isn't it?" a voice said in perfect English. "Who knew that bodies were so messy inside?"

Eckels looked around in astonishment to find the speaker. And when he saw who or what had spoken, he was even more astonished.

"What in the world are you?" he asked the apelike creature who stood grinning at his side.

"That's a good question," the creature replied. "I'm not really sure myself. I'm not this body, that's for certain. It just happens to be something I'm wearing for now."

"Uh-huh," Eckels said. He looked around, eyeing an opportunity to escape. But the press of villagers was still dense about him. Worse, the creature's presence seemed to be attracting more polite attention. The villagers crowded even closer to them and murmured about the marvel of the hairy little man. There was no way Eckels could possibly get away from it, no matter how badly he wanted to.

"Call me Mundo," the creature said. "Everybody else does." He was silent for a moment, regarding Eckels closely with his bright simian eyes. "And you're Eckels."

"That's right." There was no point in denying it. "How do you know?"

"Oh, I know some people who are looking for you," Mundo told him. "Aaron. And Travis. It seems you stole their time machine. Among other things."

"That's a lie," Eckels said automatically. His brain raced as he tried to sort out the possibilities Mundo's presence might imply. It would be trouble, Eckels realized, if this odd creature was an ally of Travis. On the other hand, if it wasn't Travis's friend, then perhaps they could come to an understanding.

"You seem pretty well informed," Eckels said in an exploratory manner. "Perhaps you can tell me what's going on here."

"Oh," Mundo said. "I've picked up a thing or two. These people are known as the Hill Makers." He gestured all around them. "You can guess why. They're enemies of the Nipponjin who've recently moved into their territory. That was one of the Nipponjin who was just sacrificed by the head priest, a fellow named Gray Raven."

Eckels nodded. He was still watching the activity on the top of the temple-mound. The ceremony over, the head priest had taken off his birdlike mask, exposing his face for the first time. It was, as Eckels had suspected, none other than Gray Hair, or Gray Raven, to use his proper name.

"This Gray Raven," Mundo continued, "is the High Priest of the Buzzard Cult. What a charming name."

"Why the sacrifice?" Eckels asked.

"Oh, the cult commonly sacrifices prisoners to the rising sun to ensure that it'll keep on rising. It's a new thing, really, gaining popularity in the village when things started going bad with the Nipponjin. The priest looks into the sacrifice's innards to tell the future—to see if the village will be successful in some future undertaking."

"Like what?" Eckels asked.

"Who cares?" Mundo said rather smugly. "I'm not really too concerned about all that. I'm interested in the time machine, myself."

"Time machine?" Eckels temporized.

"Yes, the machine you 'borrowed' from Travis. The one you've stashed around here someplace."

Eckels decided not to dispute the question of the machine's ownership for the moment. "Are you marooned in time too?" he asked.

Mundo scratched vigorously under one arm. "You bet. And I intend to get home where I can ditch this body and go back to being myself."

"Me too," Eckels said. "I mean, I'm marooned too. I see no reason why we can't work together. After all, we're both creatures of reason cast alone into this savage world."

"So where's the machine?"

Eckels looked around. The crowd was starting to disperse. The rest of the captives were being marched back into their hut. The villagers were strolling down the ramp to start their daily activities. Even the novelty of a talking ape who, after all, was not speaking their language, had worn off. Eckels and Mundo were no longer hemmed in by a mass of curious faces.

"It's outside the village," Eckels said.

"I didn't think you were keeping it in your hut," Mundo replied haughtily.

Eckels eyed his newfound companion warily. "So there'll be no trouble going after it?"

Mundo shook his head. "Me and Gray Raven are like that," he said, entwining two hairy fingers.

"I see."

He suddenly realized that he had to be very careful. He couldn't figure out how the creature managed to get on Gray Raven's good side so quickly. Eckels scented a conspiracy of some kind, a dark conspiracy whose players and motives were still mostly hidden from his view. He knew that he had to tread lightly until he could be sure exactly what was happening.

That meant he had to be nice to this ape. He could do it, but he wouldn't like it. And he certainly would exact a heavy payback when the proper time came.

"It's not far from here," Eckels said with as much enthusiasm as he could manage. "I wanted to go look at it myself, but wasn't sure if I'd be allowed to leave the village."

"You wouldn't," Mundo told him pointedly, "if you were alone."

Eckels nodded. *So that's the way it is*, he said to himself. The creature wasn't even going to maintain a pretense of equality. It was already lording it over him.

"Shall we go?" he asked.

The ape looked at Eckels as if secretly amused by something he'd said or done.

"By all means," it said politely. "After you."

Eckels fixed a glassy smile on his face. He had known the ape for only a little while and hated it already. It would be a real pleasure to get it alone in the forest where accidents could happen so easily. Where bodies could be so easily buried.

13

Captive Dragon

"Well," Jennifer said, "we may have temporarily lost Peter, but we've definitely found SStragh."

She, Aaron, and Travis stood together at one end of the citadel's garden. Captain Otomo stood with them. They were all watching Lord Akira who was sitting cross-legged on the veranda overlooking the garden. He was gazing with rapt attention at SStragh, who was wandering about somewhat disconsolately.

The sound of Jennifer's voice, or perhaps her scent, made SStragh turn suddenly to look at them. A sweet, citrus smell suddenly speared the air and SStragh raised her head, exposing her throat in joyous greeting.

"Jhenini!" the dinosaur trumpeted.

"Greetings, SStragh," Jennifer replied in the Mutata language.

Lord Akira turned to face the newcomers, his initial annoyance at the interruption tempered by a sudden thoughtfulness.

"You can converse with the dragon?" he asked Jennifer.

"Yes, my Lord," Jennifer said.

Akira continued to stare at her until she bowed deeply, respectfully, then said again, "Yes, my Lord."

"How remarkable," he said, half to himself.

"My Lord," Otomo said, after paying his respects with a bow of the proper depth, "this is a most astonishing creature. Wherever did you find it?"

"We live in astonishing times, Otomo," Akira said. "Strange storms sweep across our land, we receive visitors from the Land Beyond the Stone, monkeys walk upright and talk. Is it no stranger that we should find a dragon in the forest?"

"A dragon like those who live Beyond the Stone," Otomo murmured.

Akira spread his hands. "The Stone has existed for several years. Many times our warriors have gone to the Land of the Dragons to prove their bravery, yet never has a dragon come to us. Until now. It is an omen."

"An omen of what, Lord Akira?" Jennifer asked.

"Of great triumphs," he said. "I dream of dragons, you know. Constantly. I dream of one swooping down from the sky and carrying me upon its back home to Nippon where I appear at court to everyone's astonishment. Even the divine emperor's."

"My Lord," Jennifer said, "if I may be so bold as to point out. This dragon has no wings."

Akira looked down from the blue morning sky.

"I can see that," he said. "The dragon is a foretelling. A promise of what is to come. Now go. I wish to contemplate my dragon."

Jennifer knew that there was no sense in arguing with Akira. She looked at SStragh.

"Be patient," she said. "You're in no danger here. We'll try to free you soon."

"I wait," SStragh said simply.

Jennifer turned to Akira and bowed deeply. The others bowed with her and they withdrew from the garden, Otomo coming along with them.

"What kind of triumphs was Lord Akira talking about?" Jennifer asked the samurai captain. "Is he planning to make war on the Hill Makers?"

Otomo looked vaguely troubled. Jennifer wondered if Akira's words and manner disturbed him as much as they did her.

"He is my lord. If he has plans, I'm sure he'll tell me sooner or later . . . in the meantime, you wanted to go hunting."

"That's right," Jennifer said. "We'd like to find the man Eckels."

Travis perked up at the mention of Eckels's name. "We should have asked your dinosaur friend about him. Maybe she got him."

"Too late now," Aaron said. "But even if SStragh managed to, um, get Eckels, we still have to retrieve the time machine. Say, did you notice that someone else is missing?"

"Yes," Travis said. "Mundo."

Jennifer frowned. "I wonder what he could be up to?"

"Doesn't all that clothing bother you in this heat?" Mundo asked.

Eckels only grunted. He wanted to say, "You bother me," but he didn't dare. He couldn't antagonize the monkey until he managed to get the upper hand. Now, tramping along a forest trail with Mundo and a squad of Hill Makers, he could only sweat and keep his angry thoughts to himself. Once they reached the time machine he would have to keep on his toes and figure out how to get inside by himself. Once inside the machine they could toss all the spears they wanted. The only weapon the savages had that worried Eckels was the rifle he'd been forced to trade to Gray Raven.

But the priest hadn't come along on this jaunt. The rifle was safely back at the village, so they had nothing that could hurt him. Once he got into the time machine.

The hike to where the machine was hidden seemed to be taking a long time. Eckels had to admit that by himself he probably couldn't have found the spot again. Everything looked the same in the forest. He couldn't wait to get back to a world that had proper cities with proper buildings, proper beds, and proper food.

Suddenly they came around a hill on the forest trail and they were right on top of the clearing where he had stashed the time machine. Only now there was more than the machine in the clearing. There were also people.

A squad of samurai were poking around the bushes that concealed the craft. *Fine*, Eckels thought. He'd expected that he'd have to deal with them sooner or later. But that wasn't all. Jennifer, the stuck-up girl who'd been a captive with him back on the dinosaur world was with them. She was with a boy he had never seen before.

Eckels wondered briefly what had happened to Peter. The Gairk, he figured, had probably got him. Too bad.

He was about to slink back into the forest and have a consultation with Mundo when he saw someone else poking around the bushes that hid the time machine.

Travis.

It was Travis, damn him. How in the million worlds did he get *here*?

Travis and the others had apparently just stumbled upon the craft. They were still clearing away the protective screen of brush that Eckels had put in place just before being captured by the Hill Makers. Eckels was pondering his next move when Mundo joined him.

"What's going on?" the ape asked.

"Looks like they've found the machine," Eckels said. "You'd better stop them before they take it away. Who knows what they'll do with it?"

Mundo looked at him. "You're right," he said. He turned to the Hill Makers who had accompanied them and said a few sentences in their own language. The leader nodded and spoke to his warriors, gesturing with his war club. They all vanished into the forest. If Eckels hadn't seen them move off, he wouldn't believe they were anywhere near them.

"What're they doing?" he asked Mundo.

The ape looked vaguely troubled. "I don't know. I only told them to stop the others from taking the machine."

"You idiot," Eckels said. "They'll probably kill them."

"Kill them?" Mundo said, genuinely puzzled. "I didn't say to kill them. I just said to 'stop' them."

Eckels sighed. "You have a lot to learn about human nature," he said.

He thought hard. If the ambush succeeded, then he and Mundo would be the only time travelers left in this timeline. They and the lizard.

Eckels wasn't sure he liked that. Mundo and the lizard were both animals, decidedly odd animals. There was no way he could ever forge an alliance with them and be sure of them. This affair was a prime example of what the ape could get up to. As for the lizard, well Eckels didn't think that there was any way he'd ever understand her kind. He needed humans, like Peter, humans he could twist to his own ends. Humans he could make help find his way back home.

Humans he could get to fix the time machine.

"Damn," he said to himself. He looked around the forest. All of the Hill Makers had gone off to encircle the clearing. It seemed to be just him and Mundo. It was a risk, but Eckels decided that he had to take it.

"Look out!" he screamed. "Look to the forest! It's an ambush!"

The result was instantaneous pandemonium. Everyone in the clearing looked around, trying to locate him from the sound of his voice. Travis looked particularly perturbed.

"Eckels!" he shouted. "Are you out there?"

He slung his rifle from his shoulder, readying it for use. At almost the same moment a volley of arrows came slashing out of the underbrush. There was a chorus of horrible screams and the Hill Makers charged into the open.

The volley of arrows proved largely ineffective. Several samurai were struck for flesh wounds, but their armor prevented any major injuries. The Hill Makers had the numerical advantage, but the samurai were better armored and the Hill Makers' advantage of surprise had vanished.

The samurai responded quickly. The few who carried bows had no chance to train them on the charging Hill Makers, but they had their swords out and spears ready before the ambushers could close with them.

There were no formations or closed ranks. Each individual simply chose a foe and ran toward him. One of the Hill Makers started for Travis, but the hunter opened up with his automatic rifle and the Indian withered under the intense fire.

At the sound of the rifle's thunderous burst all combat ceased at once. Everyone, Hill Maker and samurai alike, stared in astonishment at the devastating effect the burst had on Travis's target. For a second silence reigned, then the Hill Makers went into sudden, vocal retreat. The samurai chased them, but abandoned the pursuit when the Hill Makers reached the tree line.

Eckels, watching from cover, suddenly realized that he was in big trouble. He knew the Hill Makers knew he had given them away. He doubted they would be kindly disposed toward him.

Mundo, who was watching the proceedings with fascination, started suddenly as Eckels began to move.

"Hey, what are you doing?"

"Changing sides," Eckels said over his shoulder.

He pushed through the curtain of trees and shrubs at the edge of the clearing and stepped out into the open. He began to run as fast as he could, hoping no one, particularly the Hill Makers, would notice him until it was too late.

His luck held. Jennifer was the first to see him running toward them across the clearing.

"It's Eckels," she said, pointing at him in astonishment.

Travis snarled and whirled in his direction. He pointed his rifle as Eckels skidded to a stop, looking around desperately. Caught between the arrows of the Hill Makers and the rifle of the safari guide, he wondered if he hadn't finally run out of luck.

"I've finally caught up with you, you lousy—"

But before Travis could either finish his sentence or Eckels, Jennifer pushed the muzzle of his rifle to the ground. Travis struggled, but Jennifer held onto it.

"What do you think you're doing?" she asked.

"Finishing him off!" Travis snarled.

"Who appointed you judge, jury, and executioner?" Jennifer shot back.

Eckels stood still, holding his breath, while Travis pondered the question.

"She's right, Travis," Aaron said. "We can't just shoot him down."

"He's better dead," Travis said sullenly. "He got us all into this—no telling what he'll do next!"

"Do you want his blood on your hands?" Jennifer asked quietly.

Travis couldn't meet her eyes. Suddenly, he tore the rifle out of her grasp. He took a final angry look at Eckels, then shouldered his weapon and stalked off. He was immediately surrounded by admiring samurai, who rushed up to congratulate him and touch his gun.

Eckels released the breath he'd been holding.

"Hello, Jennifer. Who's your friend?"

"This is Aaron Cofield," Jennifer said coldly. "I think you know Travis."

"Yes, we've met," Eckels said as noncommittally as possible.

The samurai started to bandage their wounds, all of which were rather minor. All of the Hill Makers had fled, except for the unfortunate warrior who had made the bad decision to charge Travis.

The leader of the samurai squad stood over the body. He drew his blade and it flashed brightly in the afternoon sun as with one blow he severed the head from what was left of the Hill Maker's corpse.

He squatted, grinning, and grasped the gory trophy by its hair. He held it out to Travis and said something, still smiling widely.

"What's he want?" Travis asked.

Jennifer stared in horrified fascination. "He says that the head is yours. It was your kill."

"I don't want the bloody thing," Travis said. "I only fired to protect our lives. I don't want to make a trophy out of it."

The samurai shrugged when Jennifer translated Travis's remark. He kept the head himself, putting it in a hide bag that hung from his sword belt.

Eckels edged toward the time machine. He had hoped to enter it during the confusion of the battle's aftermath, but the samurai were veteran troops. There was no confusion to take advantage of. Still, Eckels thought he might have had a chance to grab the vehicle and run, if only everyone kept talking.

"Going somewhere?" Aaron asked.

Punk, Eckels thought.

He turned and smiled at him. Sincerely, he hoped.

"No, not really. Close call you had there," he said jovially. "Of course, you have me to thank for warning you."

"What else do we have you to thank for?" Aaron asked.

Eckels frowned. "What do you mean?"

"If you hadn't stolen the time machine, run into this world, killed those guards at the temple—"

Eckels had forgotten about that. He knew he'd better try to smooth that over, quickly.

"That was all a mistake," he said. "Things had happened so fast that I barely could make out what was going on. I killed the guards in self-defense. I guess the priests must have got caught in the cross fire. Sorry it happened."

He could see that he was making no impression on Aaron. Jennifer was also looking rather skeptical. Nothing to do, Eckels decided, but make a run for it.

He cleared the last few feet to the time machine in a rush, and desperately pulled away the last bit of cover between him and the door.

He wrenched the door open as someone shouted orders in Japanese. He knew they were after him. He vaulted into the interior of the vehicle and was immediately cinched about the waist by a pair of powerful arms, pulled back, and flung down to the ground. He started back up, but checked himself. Six angry faces were looking down at him. Six sharp swords were drawn and pointed at various tender parts of his anatomy.

He smiled and held his hands up in surrender.

"Okay, okay. My mistake. I was a little impatient. Maybe a little bit worried. Take it easy. I won't try to run away again, I promise."

The samurai were unmollified even after Jennifer translated Eckels's capitulation. The officer in charge grunted an order and they withdrew their swords, letting Eckels get to his feet.

As he stood and dusted himself off, the officer pointed at Eckels's sword and asked an angry question.

"He wants to know," Jennifer translated, "where you got the sword."

"From Gray Raven," Eckels said. He reached for it and suddenly six blades flashed like summer lightning. Their points all touched Eckels's chest before he could close his hand on the sword hilt.

"Hey!" Eckels put his hands up in the air. "I wasn't trying anything. Honest. You can have it if you like." He gingerly reached down and pulled the sword out of the sash that held it at his waist. He handed it to the samurai. "I didn't want it, you know; Gray Raven made me take it. He traded it for my rifle."

"You gave the Hill Makers a rifle?" Aaron asked incredulously.

" 'Give' didn't enter into it. Gray Raven obviously recognized that it was a weapon. He wanted it. He took it.

He 'gave' me the sword in exchange, but do I look stupid? Would I trade a rifle for a sword if I didn't have to?"

"You're gutless," Travis spit out contemptuously.

"I suppose you would have fought them," Eckels sneered.

"Damned right."

"Then you'd be dead right now. I had no choice. Besides, it's only a lousy rifle. There's a whole rack of them in the time machine."

"Lousy rifle?" Travis repeated angrily. "Do you realize how seriously something like that can affect the time-lines."

"I don't think they can be affected any more than they've already been," Eckels said wearily. "Who cares?"

"Why you—"

Travis took a step forward, but Aaron got between them and kept them apart. Travis tried to push through him, but Aaron was adamant. Finally Travis's rage subsided.

"Hold off," Aaron said to Travis. "The authorities will deal with Eckels after we find our way home."

"I didn't do anything," Eckels said. "It was all his fault."

Aaron turned and stared him down. "Don't push your luck," he said.

The samurai officer took the sword haughtily from Eckels. The other samurai sheathed their blades, but two stationed themselves at Eckels's side, obviously ready in case he tried anything.

Travis blew out his breath in a great sigh, supressing a grimace of sudden pain. "Well," he said, "let's check the time machine and see if this idiot did anything to damage it."

He stepped toward the machine, but the samurai officer firmly planted himself in the way.

"Now what?" an exasperated Travis demanded.

The samurai spoke in level, carefully polite tones without taking his eyes off Travis's face.

"He says," Jennifer said, "that Captain Otomo told him that no one is to enter the craft until the question of ownership has been satisfactorily answered."

"Well, great," Travis said in disgust. "What do we do with it until then? Leave it here for the birds to nest in?"

Jennifer queried the samurai in somewhat more polite language.

"He says," Jennifer relayed, "that he will send someone back to the village for a team of oxen and they'll tow it back."

"This is ridiculous!" Travis exploded. "It's my machine," he said, pointing at himself for emphasis. "It was stolen by *him*. Now it's confiscated by *you*!"

"Take it easy, Travis," Aaron said softly. "We don't want to start something we can't finish. Otomo is a decent guy. You said so yourself. We'll get the ship back."

"I'm not worried about Otomo," Travis muttered. "It's that Akira who bothers me. What if he gets his sticky fingers on it?"

"We'll deal with it when the time comes," Aaron said, though that worrisome possibility had already occurred to him. "Right now let's take it easy and get back to the village in one piece. We've got the machine. We've got Eckels. Now all we have to worry about is finding Peter."

"What about me?" a cheery voice asked. "Is no one worried about Mundo?"

Aaron sighed. He turned to see Mundo grinning up at him.

Not really, Aaron thought.

But he didn't say it.

14

A Stacked Deck

Akira's audience chamber was considerably more crowded than the first time Aaron and the others had visited it, though Akira himself was not yet present. Otomo knelt to the right of Akira's throne on the raised dais in the back of the room. The samurai captain wore his formal kimono, including the red obi or sash that denoted he'd proved his bravery in the Land Beyond the Stone, and the stiff-shouldered overcoat emblazoned with the Akira *mon*, the rising sun. To Aaron he looked stern and unyielding as he knelt with his hands on his knees, his shoulders held in a stiff, straight line.

An older man, thin and frail-looking, knelt at the chair's left. He was, Aaron guessed, Akira's majordomo, the man who was in charge of the day-to-day business of the citadel. He looked wan and tired and a little confused as to what was happening.

The rest of the room was filled with samurai and men from the village. The samurai all wore their most resplendent kimonos. About a quarter of the warriors wore the red obi. A few leading farmers and craftsmen from the village, conspicuous in that they had no weapons and wore less colorful peasant clothing, were scattered among the samurai. Aaron noticed Katsu among them.

The Nipponjin crowded close together along the sides of the room, leaving the center for Aaron, Jennifer, Travis, and Eckels. Aaron wisely arranged things so that he and Jennifer knelt between Travis and Eckels. He was worried that Travis would lose his head and go after Eckels in the middle of the tribunal. Aaron had no idea what Akira would do if that happened, and he didn't want to find out. In any case, the farther apart they kept the two men, the better.

Whispered conversations rose dramatically when Aaron and the others entered the room and found a place to kneel and wait with the others. There was no doubt that they were the center of attention. Word had circulated around the village about Eckels, the man who had killed the shrine attendents, and his strange device. Most of the Nipponjin had seen it sitting under guard outside the citadel and were very excited by it. It seemed more wonderful to this nonindustrial people than talking apes or intelligent dragons.

Aaron glanced at Eckels. He looked confident and unruffled. Maybe he didn't notice the venomous glances and whispered comments that were being directed at him. Maybe he just didn't care. He was certain of his ability to manipulate people and events, but this time it seemed to Aaron that things were steamrolling out of control. Aaron only hoped that he and his friends could avoid getting caught and crushed along with Eckels.

All whispering suddenly ceased when the door behind the raised dais slipped open. Lord Akira, dressed in his gorgeously embroidered robes of state, stepped sedately into the room.

Jennifer gripped Aaron's arm. Standing behind Akira, looking as solemn and smug as he could, was Mundo. They had wondered what had happened to him. He'd immediately disappeared when they had arrived back at the village. It was obvious now that he'd gone to report to Lord Akira. It seemed that the rumors were true and somehow he had become Akira's confidant.

Looking neither right nor left, Akira solemnly paced to his thronelike chair and slowly settled himself in. Mundo followed him and crouched at his feet. Akira adjusted and smoothed his robes to his satisfaction then nodded at his majordomo, who began to speak in a thin, quavering voice.

"This tribunal," the old man said, "has been convened to conduct two separate inquiries. First, to discover who is responsible for the deaths at the Shrine of the Floating Stone. And second, to discover the truthful owners of the Steel Turtle. We shall now hear evidence relating to the first inquiry. The boy named Katsu will come forward."

Lord Akira waved his hand languorously. Katsu came out of the audience and knelt in the clear space right in front of the dais. He kept his head bowed and his eyes down and related essentially the same story he had told Captain Otomo the day before. He was nervous and ill at ease to be the center of attention and he quickly melted back into the crowd when his testimony was completed.

"Is that what the boy told you when you first met our visitors?" Akira asked, turning to his samurai captain.

Otomo nodded.

"Yes, Lord," he said, as economically as ever.

"The man named Eckels will come forward," Akira said.

Mundo translated his words and Eckels obeyed, kneeling down in the cleared space in front of the dais. Aaron thought that he was starting to look a little worried.

"What's this all about?" Eckels asked.

"You're in big trouble," Mundo told him. "Lord Akira wants an accounting for those men you killed at the shrine yesterday."

"It was self-defense," Eckels said firmly. "Tell him that."

"I will. But I don't think it'll do any good."

Mundo turned to Akira and repeated Eckels's words. Akira listened silently with something of a bored, distant expression on his face. When Mundo finished speaking he uttered a brief sentence.

"You then admit your guilt," Mundo translated.

"Wait a minute," Eckels said. "I'm not guilty of anything. It was self-defense. They attacked me first."

"It was the sentry's job," Mundo pointed out, "to guard the shrine. He was only doing his duty. The priests, of course, weren't even armed."

Eckels was looking more than a little worried. "But—"

Mundo glanced up at Akira, who looked vaguely disinterested in the proceedings, and then leapt down nimbly from the dais. He went up closely to Eckels and put a hairy arm around his shoulder in a gesture of friendly intimacy. Eckels started at the ape's touch, then seemed to steel himself into immobility. Mundo bent down and spoke quietly but intently.

"What's he saying?" Aaron whispered to Jennifer. "I can't make it out."

"Me either," Jennifer said.

"Whatever it is," Travis hissed through clenched teeth, "those two are up to no good. I feel it."

Eckels did more listening than speaking. In the end, he nodded. Mundo clapped him on the shoulder, then returned to his place at Akira's feet.

"It is the judgment of this tribunal," Akira said as if he were reading from cue cards, "that you are guilty in the matter of the deaths at the Shrine of the Floating Stone."

Mundo translated. Eckels bowed low, pressing his forehead against the tatami mat.

"I humbly acquiesce to your judgment, oh great Lord," Eckels said, "and beg for your mercy."

"This is a setup," Aaron hissed. "Something's been planned."

Jennifer and Travis both nodded.

"But what?" Jennifer asked.

Akira didn't seem surprised by Eckels's sudden change in attitude.

"You have it," he said. "Your life shall be spared. All your possessions are forfeit."

Eckels, still bowing low, backed up until he was once again among Aaron and the others.

"What was that all about?" Aaron hissed as he returned to the group.

"You'll see," Eckels said briefly. He did not look pleased.

"Now that the first question has been disposed of," the majordomo said in his quavering voice, "we shall proceed to the second: the ownership of the Steel Turtle."

Enlightenment suddenly struck Aaron.

"Oh, no," he whispered.

Once again Eckels was called to kneel before the dais.

"This object," Akira said, and Mundo translated, "known as the Steel Turtle belongs to you?"

"Yes it does, my lord," Eckels said.

Travis started to get angrily to his feet, but Aaron put a warning hand on his arm and shook his head no. Travis glared at him, but subsided as Aaron rose slowly.

"My Lord," Aaron began then stopped.

Akira looked at him expectantly. "Yes?"

Aaron was about to say that the machine belonged to them, not Eckels. But it didn't, of course. It belonged to Travis's company. He held back a sigh. Once again he found himself in the position of having to simplify things with lies. It was easy to justify in this case, but where, he wondered, would the justifications stop?

"My Lord," he began again, "the machine, the Steel Turtle, as you call it, belongs to my friend Travis. Eckels took it from us. It is not his."

Akira listened patiently while Mundo translated. Aaron glanced down at Jennifer when Mundo finished.

Jennifer nodded. "He translated your words accurately," she said. "At least as far as I could tell."

Akira steepled his fingers and looked at Aaron across the bridge they made.

"Have you any proof of ownership?" he asked.

"Proof?" Aaron asked after Mundo had once again translated Akira's words. He looked at Travis. "Is there any proof in the vehicle as to who owns it?"

Travis looked at him angrily. "Like what? A flipping registration?"

This time Aaron was unable to suppress his sigh.

"No, Lord," he said.

Akira seemed to ponder the problem for a moment, then he announced his decision which was duly translated by Mundo.

"It would seem that we have the case of one man's word against another's. As Eckels and Travis are clearly enemies, it is certain that they would not agree on this point of ownership. But which to believe? Neither has proof that he owns the Steel Turtle. But Eckels had possession of it when he appeared in our land."

Here it comes, Aaron told himself as Akira paused to let Mundo catch up in his translation.

"It is therefore my judgment that the Steel Turtle, for want of any contradictory evidence, belongs to Eckels. In accord with this tribunal's previous judgment, possession of the Steel Turtle reverts to this court as partial payment for the deaths caused by Eckels."

Akira stood. "That is all."

He turned and left the room.

Aaron's shoulders sagged. He looked at Jennifer and Travis. Jennifer, too, seemed to have realized what was going to happen. Travis, apparently taken by surprise, was stunned.

"Wh-wh-why—" he stuttered. "He can't do that! He can't take our time machine."

"He has," Eckels said flatly. "It was all planned by that monkey."

Travis's expression went from surprise to a grim frown.

"I'll take care of him," he said, starting toward the raised dais.

Aaron grabbed his arm.

"How?" he demanded. "What are you going to do?"

"That thieving rat stole our only way back home! "

"Is attacking him going to get it back?" Jennifer asked.

"In case you haven't noticed," Aaron told Travis in a low voice, "everyone is watching us. They're waiting for us to do something stupid."

"The boy's right," Eckels said sourly.

Travis took a deep breath and looked around. For the first time he noticed that none of the samurai had left the room. None had even stood. All were waiting in place, hands by their swords, with watchful expressions on their faces.

"Okay," Travis said. "But what do we do?"

"For the moment," Aaron said, "nothing. The time machine isn't going anywhere in time."

Travis nodded thoughtfully. "That's right."

"Why not?" Eckels asked.

Aaron looked at him for a long moment without answering.

"I removed some of the temporal circuitry," he finally said, "just in case something like this happened."

"Damn!" Eckels said with a laugh. "That monkey will fool around with it forever and not be able to get any-where. He'll have to come to us."

" 'Us'?" Jennifer said.

"We're all in this together," Eckels said. "Remember who saved you from the Hill Maker ambush."

"Remember who got us into this mess," Travis said darkly.

"Quiet," Aaron whispered. "Mundo's coming this way. And Eckels is right. We're all in this together. We all go home together," he said, looking grimly from Jennifer to Travis to Eckels, "or none of us do."

Travis shook his head. "I'm not—"

"Swear it!" Aaron insisted.

He put his hand out. Jennifer quickly put hers on top of it.

"I swear it. For SStragh, too."

"For SStragh. And Peter," Aaron said. He turned to Travis.

The older man stared at him for a long moment, then sighed and nodded. He put his hand on Aaron's.

"I swear it," he said, resignation and weariness in his voice.

"Absolutely," Eckels said. He put his hand on top of Travis's. "I swear it, too."

"Good," Aaron said. He pulled his hand away just as Mundo joined the group.

"No hard feelings, I hope," Mundo said. "Say. What's going on?"

"Nothing to concern you," Aaron said.

"You're mad at me," Mundo said. "Don't deny it. I know it's true."

"No one's denying it," Jennifer said in even tones.

"I had to do it," Mundo said. "Really. I had to make sure that one of us would retain control of the time machine. His High Lordness is interested in it. Too interested in it."

"And now he has it," Travis said bitterly.

"He *thinks* he does," Mundo said triumphantly. "But really I do."

"Is that so?" Aaron said. He turned his back on Mundo. "Come on, guys, we've got other things to worry about. We've got to find Peter."

Mundo moved so that he was standing in front of Aaron.

"Hey, I know this looks bad. I know it looks like I've taken everything for myself. But that's not the case. I'm still with you guys." Aaron stepped past him without saying a word. Mundo pushed in front of him again, walking backward as the time travelers marched out of the room. "Look, I'll prove it to you." He lowered his voice conspiratorially. "I know where Peter is."

Aaron stopped walking. "You better not be kidding."

"Would I kid you?" Mundo said.

"If you know, tell us."

"Okay," Mundo said. "But you're not going to like it."

"Spill it."

"Okay. He's at the Hill Maker village."

"What's he doing there?" Jennifer asked.

"Lord Akira stashed him there," Mundo said. "He . . . he saw something he shouldn't have and Akira wanted him out of the way."

"What'd he see?" Aaron asked.

"Well, he stumbled across Akira having a conference with some of the Hill Makers. They're enemies—but Akira is trying to bring both villages together. But Akira can't let it be known he's negotiating with the Hill Makers."

"You wouldn't have anything to do with this, would you?" Aaron asked darkly!

Mundo looked hurt. "Me? Of course not."

"Will Peter be safe there?" Jennifer asked.

"Sure," Mundo said.

Aaron frowned. He didn't know if they could trust Mundo to tell the truth, not with Peter's life on the line. They would have to see for themselves.

Peter's head hurt like it'd been split open, and it almost had. There was a good-size lump on the back of his skull where someone had socked him and a mass of clotted blood had dried in his hair. He wanted to clean it away, but he had neither water nor a washcloth.

He was in a hut, somewhere, probably not the Japanese village. Some other men in the hut seemed to be prisoners. They weren't in any shape to help him. Two were Japanese. One looked pretty badly hurt. He just lay there and moaned a lot. The other samurai stuck close to him.

Two other guys kept to themselves on the other side of the dark hut. They were scary-looking Indian dudes with hard, expressionless faces. They kept to their end of the hut, the samurai kept to theirs. Peter, stuck in the middle, tried to talk to both but neither understood his language, or even seemed to care.

After awhile Peter got tired of talking to himself and sat quietly, waiting. He didn't know what he was waiting for, but he had the feeling that it wasn't something pleasant.

15

A Scouting Expedition

"This is crazy," Eckels said. "I don't want to go."

"You're the only one who knows the way back to the Hill Maker Village," Aaron said. "We have to find out if Mundo was telling the truth. We have to see if they've got Peter."

Travis ran an oiled rag lovingly over the stock of his automatic rifle.

"And even if you didn't know the way," he told Eckels, "we'd bring you along anyway."

"You don't trust me?" Eckels asked in injured tones.

"That's right," Travis said. He stood, slinging his rifle over his shoulder.

Aaron turned to Jennifer. "This is going to be dangerous. Maybe—"

"Maybe I should stay behind?" Jennifer said, interrupting him.

"Well—"

"Well, nothing, Aaron Cofield. Since when hasn't this whole adventure been dangerous? I've proved that I can take care of myself. Besides, what if we need someone who speaks Japanese? Mundo's busy playing with the time machine with Lord Akira."

"The girl's right," Eckels said. "She might come in handy."

Aaron looked at Travis, who shrugged.

"All right," Aaron said. "It's just . . ."

"I know." Jennifer patted him on the cheek. "But remember, we're all in this together."

"How could anyone forget?" Eckels mumbled.

"You say something?" Travis asked.

"I said, what about him?" Eckels gestured at Katsu, who was watching the time travelers in solemn silence. "He might rat on us."

Aaron looked at the boy and shook his head. "Not Katsu."

"We should let him know what we're doing," Travis said. "At least some of it, anyway. We can't have him tagging along without knowing what he might be in for."

"You're right," Jennifer said. She turned to Katsu and told him in Japanese, "We're going to look for our friend Peter-san."

Katsu nodded solemnly. "*Hai.*"

"It might be dangerous. Mundo told us the Hill Makers have him. There might be a fight."

"Captain Otomo told me to take care of you while you are our guests," Katsu said, bowing low. "I can't disobey the captain."

Jennifer smiled and put a hand on his chin, tilting his face back so that he could look in her eyes. "You're a loyal friend, Katsu. There's no need to bow to us."

The boy nodded and smiled. Jennifer looked at the others.

"It's all set, then. Let's go."

"I still say this is crazy," Eckels said as they left the citadel. "At least we should wait for nightfall."

"Security's tighter then," Aaron reminded him. "If we wait for night, we'd never be allowed out of the village."

"Maybe," Eckels grumbled. "Maybe they won't let us leave the village now without an escort."

"We'll find out soon enough," Travis said as they tramped up to the gate.

The wooden gate in the palisade was flung wide open. It was late afternoon and most villagers were working in the paddies outside the walls. There were also work parties, accompanied by squads of armed samurai, leaving and entering the village. Some were hunting groups bringing deer, rabbits, and other small game from the forest. Woodcutters were bringing in wood for fires, charcoal makers were carrying in huge loads of briquettes to be used for cooking.

"Just look casual," Aaron said with a smile at the squad of armed guards.

But the guards didn't smile back. One planted himself in front of Aaron, his hand on the hilt of his sheathed sword.

"Told you so," Eckels said smugly as the guard barked a question at Aaron.

Aaron kept his reassuring smile and nodded at the guard.

"Guess I wasn't casual enough. What's he saying, Jennifer?"

"He's asking to see our permit to leave the village," Jennifer said with a frown.

"Great," Aaron said. "Just great."

"Even worse," Travis said. "Look who's coming."

Captain Otomo strode up to the gate, as steadfast and stern-faced as usual.

"What do you want?" Otomo asked Jennifer.

She looked back at him steadily. "To go into the forest."

Otomo looked at her for a long time. His gaze was unwavering, but so was hers. She thought that he was going to deny their request and order them back into the village when suddenly he turned to the guard and issued a single, short command.

"Let them through," he said.

"What's happening?" Eckels asked.

"Don't ask," Jennifer told him. "Just go."

The sentry stepped aside and the party hustled through the gate. Jennifer was the last to leave. She looked at Otomo and bowed.

"*Domo arigato*," she told him.

"Harrumph," Otomo said. "Just be careful."

Jennifer hurried to catch up to the others.

"He knows what we're doing," Eckels said as they strode along one of the paths that led through the verdant rice paddies.

"Maybe," Jennifer said. "He certainly knows something strange is happening. But he trusts us enough to give us our heads."

"If we screw up, he'll give Akira our heads in a basket," Eckels said.

"He won't have to," Aaron pointed out. "The Hill Makers will take care of that for him."

They passed quickly from river bottom that had been turned into rice paddies into the virgin forest. Travis, the experienced tracker, led the way to make sure that no Hill Makers were watching or following them. It was a difficult task and he was the only one with the knowledge and experience to carry it off. Any of the others would have floundered uselessly around in the bush. With Travis on point they at least had a chance of arriving at the village undetected.

The forest seemed quiet and peaceful, but Aaron knew that appearances were deceiving. There could be Hill Makers lurking behind every tree, watching their every move as they approached the village. But Travis, scouting ahead through the forest, saw no one.

Cover got scarce as they approached the village and the trees gave way to grassland and cornfields. Travis rejoined the group as they neared the edge of the forest. He took a couple of deep breaths, his hands on his hips. He looked worn out. Aaron suspected he was hurting, but he also wasn't about to admit it.

"This is where we have to be very careful," Travis said. "I've spied out the land ahead. There's an old river terrace, a bench left when the river flowed in a different channel. The bench is higher than the present river bottom and it's overgrown with brush. It'll be a good place to watch the village for signs of Peter. I don't think we can get any closer without being seen by the people working in the cornfields."

"Will we be close enough?" Jennifer asked. "Will we be able to see anything from that distance?"

"We will with this." Travis slung his rifle off his shoulder and lifted the sighting assembly from where it had been snugged down atop the receiver. He handed the rifle to Jennifer, who put it up to her shoulder and squinted through it. "The scope will make everything look like it's right next door. The field of vision isn't very large so we'll have to constantly sweep the village, but you can count the hairs on a man's chin through that thing from a thousand yards."

Jennifer nodded and handed the rifle back.

"Okay," she said. "Let's get in place on that bench of yours."

It took them most of the long, sweaty afternoon. Moving slowly and carefully, they reached the sheltered terrace after making a looping swing around the village and the fields that surrounded it.

It was a healthy hike through tough terrain. Aaron kept an eye on Travis. The tracker was hurting but uncomplaining. Eckels complained so much that pretty soon Aaron wished they'd left him behind at the Nipponjin village. But, of course, there was nothing they could do about that now.

By late afternoon they were in place, relatively comfortable and fairly secure. The river terrace was higher than the floodplain, so they could look over the earthworks and see clearly into the village below. Everyone could observe the general comings and goings, but the distance was too great to discern details or recognize individuals. The rifle scope took care of that, though, just as Travis had suggested.

"What if he's under guard in one of those huts?" Jennifer asked.

"He probably is," Eckels replied. "But they lack any, um, sanitary facilities. They'll have to let him out for that."

"Or maybe they'll let him walk around and get some exercise," Aaron offered. "They can't keep him cooped up all day."

Eckels shrugged. "Maybe."

The afternoon wore down to early evening as they all took turns on the scope, scouring the village for signs of Peter. Finally, as the tedium was rising to a snapping point and Aaron was finding it difficult to keep Travis and Eckels from each other's throats, Jennifer signaled excitedly.

"There's Peter! I see him! His hair stands out among the Indians' like a flaming torch."

"Hmmm," Eckels said with a bemused expression, "the monkey didn't lie after all."

"What's going on?" Aaron asked. "What's he doing?"

"Hard to say," Jennifer replied. "He seems to be under guard. And he's not the only prisoner. There's a samurai, and what seem to be a couple of Hill Makers."

"I got a close look at them this morning," Eckels said. "They're not Hill Makers. I think they're captives from another tribe."

"Did they treat the prisoners well when you were in camp?" Aaron asked.

"Pretty well . . . of course, they sacrificed one of the samurai at sunrise."

Jennifer looked away from the scope. "Sacrificed?"

Eckels nodded. "Cut his stomach open. The monkey told me all about it. It seems there's some kind of Buzzard Cult among the Hill Makers. They require a sacrifice to the sun every morning. Not all the villagers are members but enough are so that the cult is pretty powerful and everyone goes along with them."

"Oh, no," Aaron said softly. "We've got to get Peter out of there."

"Sure," Travis said. "But how?"

Aaron squatted down and grabbed a handful of dirt. He squeezed until his hand ached. His mind raced at full speed, but, frantic with sudden worry about Peter, he just spun his wheels. He couldn't come up with a plan to save his life. Or, he thought, Peter's.

"I don't know," he finally said, throwing the dirt down.

"Something's going on," Eckels suddenly said. "Looks like a big commotion at the gate."

Jennifer swung back to the scope.

"A cart of some kind is coming through. It's surrounded by Hill Makers," Travis said.

"That's right," Jennifer confirmed. "And Mundo's driving it."

"Mundo?" Aaron asked. "What's he up to now?"

Jennifer only shook her head.

Mundo wasn't too keen on this idea, but after all, Akira was the boss. If he couldn't talk Akira out of something, he had to obey him if he wanted access to the time machine. He'd tried his best to talk Akira out of the whole thing, but it'd been like trying to get the time machine to work. Totally useless.

Secretly loading the cart had been easy enough. No one else had been near the storeroom when Mundo removed the designated crates and stashed them where he could bring the wagon around. Getting out of the village had been simple. After all, he had Akira's personal pass. No one in the highly structured and conditioned Nipponjin society would dare question it. He even knew the way to the Hill Maker village, so getting there was no problem.

Now, though, came the sticky part.

For some reason Mundo couldn't quite bring himself to trust Gray Raven. Lord Akira had nothing but contempt for the man he considered a savage; therefore, he'd given in to the priest's request. It had seemed plausible enough on the surface . . .

But Mundo knew that Gray Raven wasn't a superficial person. He had a deep and subtle mind. He masked his thoughts so well that Akira couldn't read them from his facial expression, if Akira had been subtle-minded enough to try, which Mundo knew he wasn't. And Mundo couldn't even pick up the priest's thoughts telepathically.

He could get hints of Raven's plan, traces, really. But not enough to tell him what the priest really intended doing with the goods Akira was giving him for that damned dragon.

"You're prompt," Gray Raven told him as he met Mundo and the cart at the village gate.

"Certainly, Chief," Mundo said. "Lord Akira takes care of his obligations as soon as possible."

"That is good," Gray Raven said blandly.

Even now his mind was a closed book to Mundo's telepathic powers. Mundo could occasionally get a glimpse of a page or two, maybe even read some scattered sentences, but that was all. He couldn't see enough to make sense of what Gray Raven was really thinking. He caught misty thoughts of the Easterners, the Iroquois who had been making tentative moves into Hill Maker territory. Given Gray Raven's stated intentions, that was natural. Still . . .

Gray Raven gestured to two of the bodyguards who accompanied him everywhere he went. They clambered atop the cart. One threw off the tarp that covered the pile of crates and together they chose one of the boxes and manhandled it to the ground. One yanked the top off the crate and stepped back as Gray Raven came forward, a smile frozen on his tattooed face.

He bent down over the box and lifted out an arquebus. He held it up triumphantly over his head for everyone to see. The village broke into spontaneous cheers.

"Just as you asked for," Mundo told him, "in exchange for the dragon. Fifty arquebuses. Fuses for all, gunpowder, and two thousand rounds of ammunition."

"Thanks to your lord," Gray Raven told him, "our village will now be safe from our enemies."

"The Iroquois, you mean," Mundo said uneasily.

Gray Raven looked at him. "Of course. The Iroquois."

But in his moment of triumph, Gray Raven had allowed himself to relax. His mind had cleared. What Mundo saw was not victory over the Iroquois, at least not in the forefront of Gray Raven's mind. Not at all.

Mundo waited on the cart while Gray Raven's warriors eagerly unloaded the cases of weapons, ammunition, and gunpowder. They immediately carried everything to the temple mound and stashed it in the huts built on the mound's slopes.

Mundo waited, outwardly patient, inwardly shaking. He had to escape with his terrible knowledge and tell someone what Gray Raven planned.

But tell who? Akira, the fool, wouldn't believe him. Aaron would, but what could Aaron and his band of time travelers do?

Then it struck Mundo.

They could help him repair the time machine and get them all out of here. They had to, now.

They had to leave this world before disaster struck.

16

Conspiracy

The day had settled down to a quiet summer dusk, though Mundo was too agitated to notice the peaceful scenery through which he rode. He had no great love for the Nipponjin, but they had the time machine. If Gray Raven succeeded in his plan, that would inconvenience him greatly. Akira was easy to handle. Gray Raven might prove more difficult.

Travis suddenly stepped into the path like a ghost materializing at a seance and leveled his rifle at Mundo.

"Hold it," Travis ordered.

Mundo pulled frantically on the reins, trying to calm the normally placid horse which had reared up in fright at the sight of Travis.

"You scared me!" Mundo said accusingly. "What are you doing lurking in the forest?"

Aaron stepped onto the trail next to Travis. Jennifer, Eckels, and Katsu came out of hiding and stood on his other side.

"I can ask the same about you," Aaron said, "and the Hill Maker village."

"Village?" Mundo temporized. He looked at their faces and skimmed their thoughts. He realized there was no sense in dissembling. "Okay. I was there. Akira sent me."

"To take the Hill Makers weapons, the most advanced weapons on this world," Aaron said.

Mundo nodded.

"Why?" Jennifer asked.

Mundo shook his head. "It was that damned dragon. Akira offered the Hill Makers anything they wanted for it. Gray Raven wanted guns. He said he needed them to use against another bunch of Indians who call themselves Iroquois."

"Once he has the guns," Eckels said, "Gray Raven can use them against whomever he damn well pleases."

"That's right," Mundo said. "And he plans to use them against the Nipponjin. Soon. Maybe even tomorrow."

"Is that possible?" Jennifer said. "Won't his men have to be trained?"

"Gray Raven knows what a rifle is," Eckels said. "They probably have acquired a few here and there over the years from dead Nipponjin. It wouldn't suprise me if all the Hill Maker warriors were pretty well versed in their use—theoretically, at least."

"Didn't Akira realize the Hill Makers could use his own weapons against him?" Aaron said.

"He must have," Mundo said. "But he doesn't care."

"What do we do about it?" Jennifer asked.

Eckels shrugged. "What can we do? This is their world. Let them work out their own problems."

"We *caused* their problems," Aaron replied. "We might not've meant to add to their difficulties, but we did. We're responsible for this mess. We can't just walk away from it."

"So what's your plan, great leader?" Eckels asked sarcastically.

Aaron shook his head. "I don't have one . . . not yet."

"One thing is sure," Travis said. "We can't do anything on our own. We'll need help from the Nipponjin and we sure as heck can't go to Akira with this story."

"That leaves one person we can go to," Aaron said.

He and Jennifer said the name at the same time.

"Otomo."

They decided to send Jennifer and Aaron, along with Katsu, to speak to Otomo. Travis would stay in their quarters and keep an eye on Eckels and Mundo. Mundo at first vehemently protested the decision to keep him a virtual prisoner, but acquiesced when he realized that nobody trusted him any longer, even if he had told them where Peter was.

It took Jennifer, Aaron, and Katsu a while to find Otomo, but they finally tracked him down in the citadel's fencing hall, where he and several of the samurai were practicing with wooden swords.

Neither Aaron nor Jennifer could recognize him under the padded armor and headgear that all the samurai wore, though Katsu picked him out right away.

"That's the captain," Katsu said, pointing out a swordsman who moved like a whirlwind, devastating his opponent with a flurry of lightning-quick attacks. "I can tell by his style of swordplay."

They watched until Otomo overwhelmed his foe with thundering attacks that rattled off his opponent's armor like hail on a wooden roof. The match ended with a particularly telling blow that would have killed Otomo's partner if they had been using real swords. As it was, the sword stroke knocked the samurai over. Otomo helped him up, then they both removed their helmets and bowed.

Otomo noticed the visitors right away and headed toward them, wiping the sweat from his brow. He said something in Japanese and smiled the tight little smile that was his equivalent of a broad grin.

"Otomo-san wants to know if you'd like a bout," Jennifer said to Aaron.

Aaron shook his head with a grin. "Tell him no thanks. Maybe next time."

Otomo nodded and led them over to a wooden bench that ran the length of the fencing hall. He unlaced his thick quilted armor and Katsu helped him out of it. He sat down on the bench and looked seriously at his visitors. They began a laborious, three-way conversation that was punctuated by shouts from the fencing floor combined with the thuds and thunks of clashing wooden swords.

"You look as if there is something heavy on your minds," Otomo said.

Both Jennifer and Aaron nodded.

"It has to do with our friend Peter," Jennifer said. "But also with the welfare of your village."

"Your friend's fate is my greatest concern," Otomo said gravely. "You're my guests and under my protection. I've searched all through the citadel and village and can't find him."

"That's because," Jennifer said slowly, "he's not in the village."

Otomo looked at her, his face an unreadable block of stone. "But you've found him."

It was a statement, not a question.

"Yes, Otomo-san. He is in the village of the Hill Makers."

"Hmmm," the samurai said noncommittally.

"That's not all we saw at the village," Aaron contributed after Jennifer had caught him up with the conversation. "While we were watching for Peter, Mundo arrived at the village with a horse and cart. When the cart was unloaded, we saw that it contained arquebuses, gunpowder, and ammunition." Jennifer translated.

Otomo shot to his feet. His eyes were narrowed, his brow furrowed.

"What!" he exclaimed in an angry whisper. "Do you realize what you're saying?"

Aaron nodded solemnly. It amounted to an accusation of treason against Lord Akira. There was no way that Mundo could have brought the weapons out of the village without Akira's personal safe-conduct pass. Without it he would have been stopped, the cart searched, and the smuggled weapons discovered.

"We realize. Katsu can verify our claims. He saw everything."

The samurai turned on the serving boy. "Is this true?"

Katsu nodded. "Everything they've said."

Otomo started to pace back and forth, scowling silently, every now and then shooting angry glances at the three bearers of ill tidings. He stopped pacing after a moment and stood in front of Jennifer.

"Your claim can be checked," he said. "The armory stores are carefully inventoried. It would be the work of only a moment to verify the tallies and see if any weapons and supplies are missing."

"Check the records," Jennifer said. "You'll see that we're telling the truth."

"I will," Otomo said. "Personally. Go to my quarters and wait for me. Speak of this to no one."

"*Hai*, Otomo-san," Jennifer said with a bow.

The samurai swept them all with his hard-edged glare once more, then stalked off without a word.

"Think he believed us?" Aaron asked.

Jennifer nodded. "Oh, yes. I could see it in his eyes."

They didn't have long to wait before the samurai came into the room. His face was clouded by the fury of a hurricane barely held in check by his iron will.

"You were right," he said through lips tightly compressed in anger. "Fifty arquebuses are missing, along with several cases of gunpowder and two thousand rounds of ammunition. I checked the stores personally. No one else knows about it."

"What are you going to do?" Jennifer asked.

He looked at her. "That's the question, isn't it?"

"Gray Raven told Lord Akira that he needed the weapons to protect his village from the Iroquois," Aaron said. "But Mundo knows the chief was lying. He thinks that the Hill Makers plan to attack your village. Soon."

Otomo nodded after Jennifer had translated Aaron's words.

"Of course he will. He'll try to get rid of us first, before we learn, before *I* learn, that he has the arquebuses. Then he can worry about the Iroquois. But why didn't Akira realize this? Despite his faults, he's no fool."

"Lord Akira has never cared for village life, has he?" Jennifer asked.

Otomo snorted. "That much is obvious. He's a fop, better suited for life at court than the frontier. His brother, the *daimyo,* had hoped that this experience would change him. Would make him a useful member of the clan. But," Otomo said bitterly, "that did not seem to happen."

"If life here is intolerable for him," Jennifer said, "maybe he's found a way out."

"How?" Otomo asked. "If the village is attacked by the Hill Makers he's in as much danger—"

Otomo suddenly snapped his mouth shut and smote his forehead with the palm of his hand.

"I've been a fool!" he exclaimed. "He now has the Steel Turtle!"

"Yes," Jennifer said. "The Hill Makers can't harm him if he takes refuge inside the Turtle. He's probably planning on taking it to the settled regions of his brother's domain. Perhaps even back to the Imperial Court in Nippon."

"If the time machine has enough fuel," Aaron put in after Jennifer repeated her words in English. "Which I doubt."

"No need to mention that to Otomo-san," Jennifer said.

"True," Aaron agreed.

Otomo nodded. "I see it now. He's turned his back on us. Oddly enough, he probably won't lose much honor if he brings the Steel Turtle back to Nippon. We are only a small, rather insignificant outpost. The Turtle is a wonder. A marvel never seen before."

"As is a dragon and a talking ape," Jennifer added. "Akira's future at court would be assured."

"Yes." Otomo fell silent and started to pace again. "The question is, what to do . . . How can we counteract this terrible scheme . . ."

"Otomo-san," Katsu said respectfully. "Lord Akira is not the only one who can use the Steel Turtle."

Otomo stopped pacing and stared at the serving boy.

"Yes," he said in a faraway voice. "That is true. Katsu," he suddenly barked.

The boy bowed low, putting his forehead to the floor.

"Katsu," Otomo repeated, "if I survive this night, I will see that you get your second name."

Katsu looked up and smiled.

"If you survive, as well," the samurai added.

Katsu lost his smile, but only for a moment.

"As Buddha wills," he said.

"What's going on?" Aaron demanded.

"I think," Jennifer said slowly, "Otomo-san and Katsu are discussing the possibility of stealing the time machine."

"We can't really steal it," Aaron said. "It's ours. Or Travis's. Or at least it belongs to the company he works for . . ."

Jennifer nodded. "I get the idea. Let me see if I can confirm this with Captain Otomo."

"The Steel Turtle seems to be a powerful weapon," Otomo said. "A bold warrior might make use of it to solve all our problems."

"You mean rescue Peter from the Hill Makers and destroy the weapons Lord Akira gave them?" Jennifer asked.

"Exactly," Otomo said. "Of course, there are problems."

"Like getting hold of it?"

"Yes," Otomo admitted. "Open rebellion against Lord Akira would be foolish. Some of the samurai would follow me, but Lord Akira has his faction among the men. Some prefer his easygoing ways to my hard task-making. Anything causing open warfare between the two camps would be disastrous for the village. It could cause as many problems as an attack by the Hill Makers."

"We'd have to do it on our own."

"Mostly," Otomo said gravely. "Katsu and I will give you as much help as we can, but we can't be seen aiding you openly."

"Once we had the time machine," Jennifer said, "we could do what we have to at the Hill Maker village and then return to the Land Beyond the Stone."

Otomo nodded solemnly. "That would be best. You've been most interesting guests, but we have enough problems of our own. Your presence only adds to them."

Jennifer explained all this to Aaron, who nodded in agreement.

"It's simple," he said. "All we have to do is steal the time machine, rescue Peter from the Hill Maker village, and then destroy the weapons cache." He nodded gloomily.

"You've forgotten one thing," Jennifer told him.

"What's that?"

"SStragh. I can't abandon her. We'll have to bring her with us because there's no way we can return here after we take the time machine. We'll have burned too many bridges."

"Oh, right. So we have to steal the time machine, save the dinosaur, rescue Peter, and destroy the weapons cache. I don't see any problems? Do you see any problems?"

"Sarcasm," Jennifer told him, "is not your strong suit."

17

To the Rescue

Eckels shook his head. "I don't like this. I don't like this at all. I'm all for getting the time machine back, but this is too risky. Especially the part about going after the lizard."

"It doesn't matter what you like or dislike," Aaron told him. "It has to be done."

"You're not going to weasel out of this," Travis said meaningfully. "You caused a big part of this mess and you're going to help clean it up." He turned and looked at Mundo. "You too."

"This sounds dangerous," Mundo said sullenly.

"Oh, it will be," Aaron said. "I can promise you that."

"You're all against me because I'm not human," Mundo said.

"That's not right," Jennifer said. "It's true that you have a lot to learn about being human but no one is 'against' you. You have to earn trust and affection. It's not something we humans give lightly, especially when the trust we've given in the past has been abused."

"Listen to her, Mundo," Aaron said. "You're going to have to prove yourself worthy of trust. You can't think of yourself all the time. You have to work with us. And by doing that, you'll help yourself, too. We'll all get out of here and return home. Together."

"Do you promise?" Mundo asked.

"I can't promise," Aaron said truthfully. "I can only do the best I can to see that everything gets put back right. That's all anyone can do."

Mundo nodded. "All right." He tried not to look sullen. "I'm with you."

Aaron looked at Eckels.

"All right already. If this is the only way we'll ever get home, then I guess I'm with you, too."

"I'll be watching you," Travis promised.

"I'm scared," Eckels sneered.

"Let's not fight," Jennifer said. "We've enough to worry about without fighting among ourselves."

"Okay," Aaron said. "You know the plan. Let's get going."

They broke up into three groups. Jennifer and Katsu were going after SStragh, Jennifer because she was the only one who could communicate with the dinosaur. Katsu was going with her because he was the only one who could possibly have a legitimate reason for being around SStragh.

Mundo and Travis were going after the time machine. Mundo still had Akira's personal pass. That would give them access to the machine. Travis was accompanying him because he had the most experience with the machine and he could get it out of the village with the least fuss.

Aaron, Eckels, and Otomo headed for the gate. They didn't want to go with Mundo and Travis because a big group was liable to make the sentries suspicious. They planned to leave the village on the pretext of hunting for Peter. Otomo would be their pass. The sentries at the gate wouldn't question an expedition he was leading.

Before they separated, Aaron and Jennifer hugged fiercely.

"Take care," Aaron said. "Be careful."

"We will," Jennifer promised. "You be careful, too."

"Right." Aaron turned to Travis and took his hand. "Watch yourself."

"We've got the easy part," Travis said. He unslung his rifle and handed it to Aaron. "Here. Take this."

Aaron looked at the weapon dubiously. "I don't know, Travis . . ."

"I do," Travis said. "There's no reason for me to take it into the machine. There's every reason for you to have it when you leave the village."

"If the boy doesn't want it, I'll take it," Eckels said.

Aaron slung the carrying strap over his shoulder. "I'll take it."

"Fine," Eckels sniffed.

"Good luck to all," Aaron said with a wave as he, Eckels, and Otomo started for the village gate.

The sun was setting as Jennifer and Katsu arrived in the citadel's garden. It was deserted but for SStragh, who was lounging disconsolately by the fish pond, watching the flashing bits of color dart under the cool, clear water. Akira had confiscated her spear. She had known better than to argue, even if she had been able to speak their language. But losing the weapon meant a lot. There was no pretext of her being a guest. She was even less than a captive in Akira's eyes. She was an animal in a zoo, a pet, a gaudy treasure. It made her feel sad and despondent.

"Jhenini!" SStragh trumpeted at the sight of her friend. "It seems so long since I've seen you!"

"I know. It seems long to me, too. But don't worry. We've come to take you with us. We're leaving the village."

Jennifer quickly filled SStragh in on their plan to capture the time machine and use it to rescue Peter.

"We have to get you out of here," Jennifer said, "and meet Aaron, Captain Otomo, and Eckels, who're waiting for us outside the village."

SStragh's crest rose with anger at the mention of Eckels's name.

"Eikels, my enemy," she said. "You have captured him."

Jennifer shook her head. "Not captured. He's working with us. We're all working together to find a way out of this mess."

"He is my enemy," SStragh said. "He killed members of my tribe. I must avenge them."

"I know he's done terrible things," Jennifer said, "but any retribution must wait."

"That is not the OColihi," SStragh said and realized what she was saying just as the words came out.

"It's time for the OColihi to change," Jennifer said. "You know that yourself."

"Yes . . ." SStragh acknowledged.

Jennifer could see that the thought was distressing SStragh, even though she had been championing that very philosophy ever since Jennifer had known her. It was easy, Jennifer thought, to think such a thing, but very difficult to act on it.

"We'll worry about that later," Jennifer said before SStragh could sink too low into despondency. "Now let's worry about getting out of here."

"Do you have a plan?" SStragh asked.

"Not much of one," Jennifer admitted. "We'll smuggle you out of the garden. Katsu knows some ways out of the citadel that are unguarded. Once in the village we'll go under the wall where the millstream flows down to the river, where Aaron and Captain Otomo are waiting."

"Oootumooo?" SStragh asked.

"He's the samurai captain—and he's on our side. I'll explain later. Now—"

Jennifer fell silent as she felt Katsu tug her sleeve. She glanced at him and with shifting eyes as he gestured toward the veranda that overlooked the garden. Jennifer followed his gesture and her heart sank.

Lord Akira was sitting in his usual place on the veranda, silently watching them. She had no idea how long he'd been there. Fortunately she and SStragh had been conversing in the Mutata tongue, so Akira could have no idea what they'd been saying. But his mere presence was enough to upset their plans.

She knew that he knew that she knew he was there. So she did the only thing she could. She bowed low, Katsu following suit at her elbow.

"Lord Akira," she said.

He nodded languidly to acknowledge her presence.

"Jennifer. How good to see you again. Have you been enjoying your stay in our domain?"

"Very much, Lord."

"Excellent. I find it a boring place myself, with little culture and few opportunities for civilized conversation."

Jennifer nodded. There wasn't much she could say in reply to that. Not much she dared say, anyway.

"I was just listening to you converse with my dragon. Is it a very intelligent creature?"

"As intelligent as you or I, Lord."

Akira nodded. "Perhaps. It has a remarkable-sounding language. Even more barbaric than the tongue of the natives of this forsaken land."

"She, my Lord."

"Eh?"

"Her name is SStragh. She's a female Mutata."

"Mutata?"

"That is what her people call themselves."

"How remarkable," Akira said. "There's much I would learn of her and her land." Akira gestured that Jennifer should sit down. "You will translate my questions and i— that is, her—answers."

Jennifer dipped her head in a brief bow. There was nothing she could do but hope that Akira had a short attention span.

"Yes, my Lord," she said.

Three armed sentries guarded the time machine as it stood as still as a statue on the open ground in the village center. Most of the excitement concerning it had died down. There were no longer any crowds gazing at it in awe, for, after all, it hadn't moved or done anything inter-esting all day. Most people had gone to their homes for the evening rice.

Travis and Mundo watched the sentries for a moment. They didn't seem overly concerned about their task. They were squatting together, gesticulating and shouting as they tossed something on the ground at their feet. Their spears leaned against the machine's hull some feet away. They were deeply engrossed in their game, hardly worried that someone would come along and try to heist the prize they were guarding.

"Let's do it," Travis said.

Mundo reached out a furry paw and put it on Travis's arm, holding him back.

"Do you know what fear feels like?" he asked the hunter.

Travis frowned, looking down at his companion. "Sure I do. Ever face a charging T-rex, bigger'n a building, moving faster'n anything human, teeth the size of sword blades and a mouth the size of a small cave?"

Mundo shook his head.

"And that's not all. The thing smells like fear—its breath rotten with the stench of decayed meat, its hide caked with putrid swamp mud. It sounds like your worst nightmare with its angry, hungry voice. And you know that if you make a mistake, if your brain freezes and your finger seizes on the trigger, or even if a single drop of sweat drips from your brow and gets in your eyes and ruins your aim, the thing will be on you before you can blink. And with a single snap of its jaw it can rip you right in half and you'll be down its gullet before you even stop thinking."

Mundo nodded, impressed by Travis's description.

"Does everyone know fear?" he asked.

"Everyone who's smart does."

"I never knew fear for all the years of my existence, until I found myself trapped in this small, frail thing you call a body. Now I know fear all the time. It tears at me constantly. It consumes my every moment. I now know what fear is—and shame."

Travis looked at him with his cool, clear eyes.

"It's not shameful to be afraid," Travis said. "It's only shameful to do bad things because of your fears. You may never be able to conquer fear, but you can learn to live with it."

"Can I?" Mundo asked.

"Most people, most thinking beings, can. Otherwise, you become like Eckels."

Mundo nodded. "I see, I think." He sighed. "Having a body is more difficult than I ever dreamed it would be. Okay. As you said, let's do it."

Mundo took a deep breath and he and Travis stepped out into the open. They were within ten feet of the time machine before the sentries noticed them. The one who saw them first leapt to his feet, snatching the helmet he'd taken off and put on the ground next to him. He grabbed for his spear, but missed it. It slid down the hull, clattering against the other spears. They all fell to the ground.

The other sentries leapt up, concerned looks on their faces. One grabbed a handful of dice and stuffed them into his pocket. Then he reached for his spear, trying to untangle it from the pile on the ground.

"Relax," Mundo said as casually as he could. "It's only me. Brought Travis along to take a look at the, uh, Turtle here. See if we can get it to work right."

The sentries were visibly relieved when they realized that it was only Mundo and not Akira—or worse, Captain Otomo. They glanced at each other and the one nominally in charge finally spoke.

"Lord Akira has said that no one is to go into the Steel Turtle without his personal supervision."

"He didn't mean *me*," Mundo said.

The sentries looked unconvinced.

"Otherwise," Mundo added, producing the clinching argument, "he wouldn't have given me this."

He held out the scroll with Akira's personal seal on it. The sentries peered at it in the waning light and finally the sergeant nodded.

"All right," he said. "But do not make the Turtle move."

"Why would I do want to do that?" Mundo asked disingenuously.

The sergeant shrugged.

"It'll be all right," Mundo said. "Go back to your game."

The sentries at least had the grace to look guilty as Mundo and Travis climbed into the time machine.

The third group had no problems at all getting out the front gate. Otomo saw to that. The sentries saluted smartly as he, Aaron, and Eckels sauntered out past the palisade into the open.

The rice paddies were practically deserted, though there were still a few of the more determined, or overworked, farmers weeding their allotments in the declining light. A few others were straggling home after a hard days' work.

"It's beautiful," Aaron said, though of course he knew that Otomo couldn't understand him. "Beautiful and peaceful."

"If you can forget about the Hill Makers," Eckels said.

"True," Aaron sighed. There was no such thing as Eden, he realized. Every place had its problems, problems that would get worse if the timelines continued to unravel. There had to be a way to stop the process.

They walked out among the paddies until no one else was in sight, then Otomo quickly led them into cover. They ran for a copse of trees that was close to the river's edge and then followed the samurai captain as he led them on a circuitous route taking them back to the village palisade, out of sight of the sentries.

Otomo said something and pointed at a small stream that ran through the village down to the river proper.

"This is it," Aaron said. "The millstream. If everything goes right, Jennifer and Katsu should bring SStragh along any time now." He looked at the sky. There wasn't much daylight left. "Any time at all."

18

Or Maybe Not

Travis sat down and felt the old, familiar contours of the driver's chair enfold him. He reached out and caressed the controls lovingly. Being back in the time machine felt, momentarily, like being home again. But the warm waves of nostalgia were quickly washed away by the harsh realization that his home reality was lost somewhere in the tangled strands of time and he probably would never find his way back there again.

Travis slumped in the chair. Mundo looked at him searchingly as he grimaced, his face hardening as the sad, familiar feelings of loss and loneliness threatened to overwhelm him.

"What's wrong?" Mundo asked.

"Nothing," Travis said briefly. "Nothing I can fix, anyway."

Now it was Mundo's turn to look concerned.

"Is the machine broken? Did I do something bad to it?"

Travis roused himself and sat up straight. He turned on the power and glanced over the control board.

"Nothing much—though the way the controls are set you'd shoot straight up into the sky and go into a power dive when you reached an altitude of a thousand feet. Three hundred miles an hour straight into the ground."

Mundo gulped as Travis suppressed a smile. It wasn't quite as bad as all that, though Mundo had monkeyed the controls some. Travis was exaggerating a bit—well, more than a bit. But it would do Mundo some good to have a little humility scared into him.

Travis felt the machine come alive around him. Power thrummed like the warning growl of a great beast. He balanced the thrust vectors and grabbed the stick. He looked over at Mundo who was sitting in the codriver's seat.

"Strap yourself in, son. Time to show these fellows what we can really do."

Travis's feeling of overwhelming helplessness dissipated as he drank in the thrumming power building around him. He flipped the machine into flight mode and gunned the accelerator.

"Yyyyeeeeowwwww!"

The time machine rose swiftly on its jets and screamed off into the gathering night. One moment it was there, the next it was gone. The three sentries looked up from their dice game as a sudden hot wind blew over them. Their jaws dropped. They looked at each other, none believing what they'd just barely seen.

"Buddha preserve us," one finally said.

"He'd better," the sergeant said. "Who's going to tell Lord Akira?"

The time machine rose into the sky like a meteor in reverse, with a roaring scream that had never before been heard in this world.

Jennifer heard it in the citadel's garden and knew what it meant. SStragh might have guessed, but Katsu and Akira were mystified. Akira, though, was smart enough to connect the unknown sound with his mysterious visitors.

"What was that noise?" he asked Jennifer politely, almost idly.

"I don't know, Lord," she said steadily.

"Perhaps not," he murmured. He clapped his hands twice and a squad of armed samurai appeared instantaneously from where they had been stationed in the room that opened onto the garden veranda. He spoke to them without taking his eyes off Jennifer. "Goro, take two men and check on the Steel Turtle. You other two men, stay here."

"Katsu," Jennifer said quietly so that Akira couldn't hear, "you must go to Otomo and Aaron and tell them we couldn't get away."

"Come with me," Katsu pleaded in a whisper.

Jennifer put her hand on Katsu's shoulder. "All right. We'll try."

"Is there something I should know?" Akira asked with an edge in his voice.

Jennifer smiled. "Many things, my Lord. Perhaps someday enlightenment will come." She switched from Japanese to Mutata. "SStragh! Come on, now!"

The dinosaur was on the other side of the garden. Alert and quick-thinking as always, she obeyed Jennifer's order instantaneously. Moving faster than any human could ever dream to, she jumped across the small stream that trickled out of the fish pond and was at Jennifer's side before Akira could leap to his feet and shout orders.

Katsu, Jennifer, and SStragh dashed to the far side of the garden, following the stream, as Akira screamed orders at his samurai. The two warriors leapt from the veranda and chased them, drawn swords in their hands.

Katsu was in the lead. He threw himself on his belly into the stream where the citadel wall met the flowing water. He clawed at the rocks and streambed silt and pushed through under the wall. He turned, stuck his head back into the garden, and called out to Jennifer.

"Come on, we can make it!"

"No," Jennifer told him as the samurai closed in. "SStragh will never push through the tiny gap between the wall and the streambed. I can't desert her again. Tell Aaron and Otomo-san that Akira has us. Tell Aaron—"

"Jhenini!" SStragh called out in a trilling warning.

Jennifer glanced back. The samurai were almost on them.

"Go!" she ordered Katsu.

The boy hesitated, agonizing.

"*Hai!*" he finally said, and disappeared.

Jennifer turned back to face the samurai. They were both young. Neither wore the red obi that said he had been to the dinosaur world beyond the Floating Stone. Now that they had caught Jennifer and SStragh, they didn't seem to know what to do with them. Both had their swords out, but neither seemed anxious to come in too close.

SStragh was unarmed, but still a frightening sight. Her crest was erect and she was exuding the sour odor of challenge and threat. Her head swayed back and forth on her long, sinuous neck, her eyes unblinking as she stared first at one, then the other samurai. She hissed like a steam engine, her taloned hands opening and closing spasmodically, her tail whipping back and forth like a great snake.

Jennifer stepped forward and put her hand on SStragh's scaly shoulder.

"There's no need for violence," she told the samurai. "We won't resist you."

The samurai glanced at each other and nodded. They sheathed their swords. One stepped forward, obviously going into the stream to follow Katsu. Jennifer stepped in front of him.

"But we won't let you go after the boy, either," she said in a flat, final voice.

The samurai looked at her and seemed to think things over.

"All right," he finally said gruffly. "What does a serving boy matter, anyway. Come with us."

Jennifer turned to SStragh. "I'm sorry we didn't make it."

"You could have escaped," the Mutata told her.

"No I couldn't," she said, shaking her head. "I couldn't desert you. You're my friend."

"I see," SStragh said wonderingly. "I see."

Katsu went down the stream as fast as he could. Every moment he expected to hear a cry raised behind him, or feel a sword point or arrow tip pierce his back. But there was nothing. No sound of alarm, no trace of pursuit. This pushed him to an even greater effort as he was consumed with sudden fear for Jennifer and her strange friend, the dragon.

The pond stream joined with a bigger stream that gave the villagers fresh water and provided power for the mill that was inside the village walls. The water in this rivulet was almost deep enough to hide Katsu as he half swam, half pulled himself along its bottom. Fortunately the rocks that lined the streambed had been smoothed by centuries of flowing water, but they still bruised his knees and palms when he came down hard upon them.

Katsu ignored the pain and pushed on grimly. Finally he saw the village palisade looming before him in the gathering darkness. He felt for the gap between streambed and wall bottom. It was narrow, but the silt on the streambed was soft and muddy. He dug with clawed fingers until there was room enough to squeeze through.

He went under the wall. He was stuck for a moment, but the thought of being pinned there until he drowned gave him enough panicked strength to push himself through. He shot through the gap like a melon seed squished between thumb and forefinger and broke the water's surface gasping for air.

He looked around wildly. It was night. The moon hadn't risen and there was no light by which to see. For a moment panic returned and then he heard someone hissing from a nearby stand of bushes. He splashed across the stream and threw himself on the bank, gasping for breath.

In a moment he was surrounded by three figures. His heart flipped wildly, then he recognized Otomo-san, Aaron, and the man called Eckels. They pulled him up into cover.

Aaron was questioning him, but of course Katsu couldn't understand a word he was saying. He seemed worried, though, and he kept glancing back at the stream as if expecting Jennifer and her dragon friend to pop up at any moment.

"Otomo-san," Katsu said when he could get his breath, "Jennifer-san and the dragon remain in the citadel. Lord Akira has them under guard."

Otomo nodded gravely. Aaron looked from Katsu to Otomo, growing more agitated by the moment. The man Eckels stood aside, aloof, almost uninterested. Aaron at last realized that he had to talk simply and slowly to get any kind of point across.

"Jennifer?" he asked.

Katsu shook his head.

"Akira," he said, and pointed back toward the village.

Aaron seemed to understand. He nodded once, grimly, and started away from the group. Otomo stopped him before he could take more than a step, holding his right arm in a grip of iron. Aaron made a single move to pull away, his eyes full of sudden anger. But Otomo held him with a strength the younger man couldn't hope to over-come. For a moment Aaron stared at him angrily.

"Peter-san," Otomo said, pointing toward the forest, and all the rage seemed to drain out of Aaron.

Otomo let go of his arm. Aaron looked back at the vil-lage wistfully, almost pleadingly. When he turned and looked back at Otomo, Katsu could see that his face had taken on some of the hardness that was Otomo's habitual expression.

Aaron, Katsu realized, had grown from a boy not much older than Katsu himself to a man others would follow, much like Otomo. Otomo seemed to know it too. He nodded at Aaron and lightly clapped him on the shoul-der. Together they moved into the forest. Eckels followed with a secretly amused looked on his face.

Katsu stood and took his position at the rear of the group.

Travis and Mundo were waiting with the time machine in the rendezvous spot, a forest clearing partway to the Hill Maker village.

The moon had risen, bringing some light to the night. They recognized the party immediately as they came out of the forest. Travis lifted an arm in greeting and hailed them with a glad cry as they approached.

"Aaron, boy! You made it! Great—" but he broke off as he saw the grim look on Aaron's face. At the same moment he realized that the group wasn't complete. "Where's Jennifer? And her dinosaur?"

Aaron shook his head.

"They didn't make it. I don't know what exactly happened. Mundo, get the story from Katsu."

Mundo nodded, responding automatically to the unquestioning tone of command in Aaron's voice. The story was told and translated in quick order.

"I wouldn't worry too much," Travis said, though there was worry in his own voice. "I don't think Akira would hurt Jennifer."

"I don't think so either," Aaron said grimly. "But who knows for sure? He's an unpredictable, probably vindictive, man. Maybe we should take the machine and go back for her right now."

Eckels shook his head. "I don't think I'd like to tackle a whole village of samurai."

"Who cares what you think?" Aaron blazed at him.

Travis suddenly found himself in the unaccustomed role of peacemaker.

"Let's not go off half-cocked," he said. "Our sudden appearance might put Jennifer in more danger than she's in now. Listen, why don't we ask Otomo what he thinks Akira will do? He knows Akira a lot better than we do."

Mundo put the question to him. Otomo thought it over for a moment, rubbing his chin as he paced. He finally stopped and looked at the others. Mundo translated his words as he spoke.

"This is what I think," the samurai captain said. "I don't believe that Jennifer-san is in any danger. Akira is many things, but he's no fool. He knows by now that the Steel Turtle is in your hands. He knows it's a potent weapon. If he's at all concerned for his safety—and that is always paramount in his mind—he knows that you won't be kindly disposed toward him if he harms your friend. The only hope he has of salvaging anything from this situation is to use Jennifer-san as a bargaining piece. Therefore, she's safe.

"But if we attack the village, there's no telling what may happen in the heat of battle. Jennifer-san could easily be harmed inadvertently. Also, though I believe Lord Akira should be deposed for his treason, I've no wish to fight my own people if it can be avoided.

"My counsel is to rescue your friend Peter-san from the Hill Makers and then attempt to negotiate Jennifer-san's freedom."

Everyone took a moment to think over Otomo's words.

"Sounds like a good plan to me," Eckels finally said.

Travis looked up at him. "Much as I hate to agree with anything Eckels says, I agree with this."

Aaron nodded and looked at Mundo.

"Yes," Mundo said. "Yes. This sounds best to me."

"Ask Katsu what he thinks."

"Okay," Mundo said, and put the question to the serving boy in Japanese.

"Me?" Katsu asked, plainly astonished that he was being consulted in the matter.

Aaron didn't need a translation to understand his reaction.

"Tell him we're all in this together," he said to Mundo. "Tell him we all help make the decision."

Mundo did so. Katsu looked wonderingly at them all, lastly at Otomo, who nodded gruffly.

"A wise commander consults all his knowledgeable warriors before making his final decision," Otomo told him.

Katsu felt that his chest would burst with pride.

"Let us then snatch Peter-san from under the noses of the Hill Makers, then demand the return of Jennifer-san from our dog lord."

"Agreed," Aaron said.

19

Six Against Six Hundred

Peter had never had a longer or more unsettling night. The samurai with the severe arrow wound died early in the evening. Stoic until the end, he had made no sound or complaint until his final breath rattled in his throat. It was a horrible thing to hear. Nobody came into the hut for the body. Peter had a difficult time sleeping with the corpse so near. Finally, after hours of tossing and turning, he drifted into a light, dream-haunted sleep that was broken when someone shook him not too gently by the shoulder.

He awoke to find one of the Hill Makers standing over him, his tattooed face a hideous mask peering down at him from inches away. He barely managed to stifle a scream. The Hill Maker shook him again, pulled away his hide blanket, and gestured for him to get up.

"All right," Peter said querulously. "Keep your shirt on."

It was cold in the hut and still dark. The Hill Makers marched Peter, the remaining samurai, and the other two Indians out of the hut without a second glance at the stiff corpse resting uneasily under its scrap of blanket.

191

The sun had not yet risen. The village was still enveloped in the mists of predawn. But that hadn't kept everyone from crowding around the top level of the mound where Peter and the others had been imprisoned. The whole village seemed to be present, waiting with an air of expectant anticipation.

Peter didn't like the way things were shaping up. He liked things even less when the gray-haired guy to whom he had been delivered the day before walked through the doorway of the other hut on the mound's upper level.

He was a hard-faced, scary-looking dude. He had a long, wicked-looking knife chipped out of something that looked like black glass. And he was looking right at Peter.

"What's going on here?" Peter demanded. "What are you guys going to do?"

A Hill Maker warrior had him by each elbow. Peter towered over most of the Indians, but these two were his height and had hard, strong-muscled bodies. They started to drag him toward the chief, who was waiting impassively by a block of dark stone that looked suspiciously like an altar of some kind.

"Now wait just a minute here!" Peter cried, but they ignored his protests and continued to drag him along.

Panic lent Peter sudden strength. He twisted, pulling the man holding his right arm, and brought his knee up hard into the man's groin. The Hill Maker grunted in pain. He let go of Peter's elbow and fell to his knees.

Peter whipped his free hand up and around and smashed his palm against the other guard's jaw. The Hill Maker grunted and his head snapped back, but he held on grimly to Peter's arm and tried to trip him.

Peter was having none of that. Calling upon knowledge gleaned from his karate training, he struck his opponent hard in the solar plexus. The Hill Maker fell upon his fellow guard.

A wave of wild exultation swept over Peter and he danced away from his foes. He stepped backward and bumped into the Hill Makers who were still holding the samurai prisoner. They were looking at him with astonishment, as if bewildered at Peter's resistance. The samurai watched with dull, fatalistic eyes.

"Come on," Peter shouted at his fellow prisoner. "Make a break for it! Come on!"

For a wild moment he considered freeing the samurai from the clutches of his captors, but he saw fatalistic acceptance in the man's eyes and knew that he wouldn't help.

Peter whirled, dodging one of the Hill Makers, who was only now slowly reaching for him. He took three steps to the edge of the mound, and stopped.

He looked out on a sea of faces that was staring up curiously at him. There were hundreds of Hill Makers. Even now some of the men were pushing through the crowd, trying to reach the level of the mound where Peter stood. Curiously, most of the villagers were just watching, as if unwilling or unable to step onto the mound's upper level.

Peter noticed that the men pushing through the crowd were tattooed and dressed like the guards. Perhaps the top of the mound was consecrated ground and only certain men could step on it. Whether that insight was correct or not, Peter realized that it still wasn't going to do him much good. There were still more than enough of the tattooed geeks to handle him. There was no way he was going to escape.

He choked back a snarl of frustration and caught his breath with a sudden gasp. He wasn't going to break down, he told himself, he wasn't. He backed away as the guards surrounded him.

"All right," he said aloud. "You've got me. But I'm not going easy."

He resumed a fighting stance, his panted breath fogging in the cold dawn air.

As the guards warily approached a sliver of sun broke over the horizon. Part of Peter noted the edge of the molten red ball as it slipped over the trees. It was a beautiful sight. He thought of a line in a movie he had seen once, and was irrationally irritated that he couldn't remember the name of the picture.

"It's a beautiful day to die," he said.

The first Hill Maker reached for him and Peter took him down with a beautifully executed side-kick.

Something big and black and fast suddenly came at them right out of the rising sun. At first, the part of Peter's mind that wasn't concentrating on fighting thought it was a bird. But a bird had never been shaped like that, nor did one ever move so fast.

It was upon them like a thunderbolt, cutting through the sky like a knife. The Hill Makers, every one of them, looked up and stared in total astonishment. Some screamed and panicked. The crowd massed around the base of the mound's upper level broke.

The machine—it was a machine, Peter realized, probably the much-prized time machine that everyone had been after—turned and came back for a second pass.

This time it dived right over the crowd, passing a scant foot or two over their heads. Terror took complete control. People ran screaming down the sides of the mound. Some fell and rolled down the steep slopes. Others were simply trampled underfoot. Some ignored the fact that the upper precincts were off-limits to commoners and swarmed over the top level, pushing between Peter and his opponents.

The machine looped back and stopped on a dime. It hovered six feet above the surface of the mound's top level. A door opened silently like a great unfolding wing and Travis stuck his head out of the machine. He had an automatic rifle on his shoulder.

"Aaaaaayyyyeaaahhhhhh!" he screamed. Then he triggered the weapon.

He fired a long ratcheting burst, aiming several feet above head level, but the panicked crowd didn't realize that.

Aaron popped his head out the door, half-behind Travis.

"Peter!" He shouted, waving frantically. "Come on, man, come on!"

Peter had never been so happy to see his onetime friend. And he didn't need any more encouragement. He started to run toward the machine.

Aaron stuck his head back inside and shouted directions. "Lower it! Get down another couple of feet!"

Peter had to cover twenty yards to reach his rescuers. It was the greatest twenty yards of broken-field running he ever did in his life. His way was blocked by dozens of running, screaming people who were milling in a frenzied panic and he was being chased not by an angry defensive back but by half a dozen Hill Makers who had remained focused on their goal of capturing him.

As he dodged screaming children and hurdled fallen, trampled bodies, his eyes were focused straight ahead on his goal. One of the Hill Makers came at him from the front. He tried to grab Peter, but Peter gave the surprised warrior a classic stiff-arm and knocked him flat on his back.

Someone then grabbed his shoulder from behind, but Peter twisted, shrugged, and broke free from the clutching hands. He was almost home, panting from exertion and the adrenaline running through his system like a train gone wild.

Aaron was reaching down to help pull him up into the cockpit of the machine and Travis was still screaming like a madman and adding to the panic by firing into the air. Peter reached out to take Aaron's hand and Travis suddenly stopped yelling nonsense and shouted, "LOOK OUT!"

Something like an angry swarm of bees buzzed past Peter's head. Several of the things slapped against the machine's hull and ricocheted off with hurt, angry whines. Aaron fell backward with a cry. Travis leveled his rifle with a gritted curse. Peter felt something smack him in the chest and he staggered, tripped, and went down.

What happened? he thought dully. He put his hand on his upper chest and drew it back, covered with blood.

I've been shot, he thought. *How did that happen?*

A voice shouted inside the machine, "Let's get out of here!"

He recognized that voice. It was Eckels. The jerk. He'd tried to abandon him once before. But Peter had fooled him. He'd climbed out of the chimney. He had done it once and he could do it again. He tried to climb, but for some reason his legs wouldn't move.

He'd turned when he had fallen, so now he was facing away from his rescuers. His eyes could barely focus, but looking back toward the altar he saw that the gray-haired priest had got a rifle from somewhere. It looked like Eckels's rifle. The priest was aiming it at them.

He must have shot me, Peter thought.

"Hold it steady!" Travis roared as the machine bounced like a feather tossed on the wind.

There was a long, long moment as if time had stopped. The Hill Maker stood still as he aimed the automatic rifle. Peter felt angry. He had come so close to getting away.

Someone jumped down from the machine hovering above him, landing next to Peter with a thud. It was Katsu, the Japanese boy.

"Peter-san!" he shouted, adding some other gibberish. He hooked his arms around Peter's chest and heaved. In a remarkable show of strength he pulled Peter to his feet, but then he suddenly sagged against Peter and they both went down, Katsu on top of him. Peter put his hand against the boy's back. It was wet. Very wet.

Travis screamed again, a long, wordless cry of anger and pain, and snapped off a single shot. Peter struggled to sit, his brain telling him dully that he had to get himself and Katsu out of there before the priest could fire again. But even then part of him realized that it was too late for at least one of them.

Someone else dropped down from the vehicle, a short, hairy someone who lifted Katsu and Peter easily, one in each arm, and hauled them up into the cockpit of the machine.

Peter looked back as he was handed up. The priest was sprawled across his altar, the rifle lying in the dirt at his feet.

Inside the vehicle was a crazy, confused scene. Aaron was fighting the controls, blood streaming from a wound in his right arm. Apparently he'd been clipped by a slug from the same burst that had got Peter.

Eckels was crouched against the far wall while Otomo held the naked point of his sword against Eckels's throat. Eckels looked more scared than angry. Otomo looked very much like he wanted to use his sword.

Mundo put Katsu gently down on the floor behind the driver and codriver seats. A series of wounds had stitched across the boy's back. Peter had been lucky. The bullet that had hit him in the chest had first ricocheted off the metal body of the vehicle and was nearly spent when it had struck Peter. Katsu had taken a burst straight on.

Travis leaned back into the cockpit and slammed the door shut. He looked down at Katsu, a stricken look on his face.

Katsu murmured something, his face screwed into a grinning grimace.

"What did he say?" Aaron asked.

"He wants to know," Mundo said in a small voice, "if he has earned his second name."

Otomo glared at Eckels, who cowered in the corner. He strode forward, then knelt down before the boy.

"You have," Otomo said in a quiet, gentle voice.

He handed his sword hilt-first to the boy. Katsu took it, wonder and gratitude in his eyes. Otomo bowed low, his forehead touching the deck. When he looked up again the boy was smiling. His eyes were glazed and unseeing.

Otomo took a moment to arrange Katsu's hands so that he held the sword clutched upon his breast. Then he looked up, his face as hard as ever.

"We're not done here yet," he said. "Where did Gray Raven store the munitions Akira sent him?"

Travis pointed through the front viewscreen. "Right there. In the same hut he got the rifle from."

Otomo nodded. "Take us there."

Travis took over the controls from Aaron, who was busy tying a bandage around his upper arm.

"Hurt bad?" Peter asked him.

Aaron looked up at him. "Not as bad as you seem to be."

"I don't know," Peter said. "It doesn't seem so bad. Maybe I'm in shock."

Aaron, finished bandaging his wound, leaned over Peter, who was sitting tiredly against the cabin wall.

"Mine was just a graze," Aaron said. "Looks like you took a direct hit."

He examined Peter's chest. An entrance wound was near the collarbone and the exit wound was through the muscle and flesh of his shoulder blade.

"You took your time getting here," Peter said. "A few more minutes and I'd've been a goner."

Aaron smiled down at him. "We had it under control all the time. We knew you were in the village last night. We just weren't exactly sure where they were keeping you. We knew we had just one chance to get you out. We couldn't afford to go into the wrong part of the village. So we had to wait until they brought you into the open. Now hold still while I take a look at you.

"Hmmmm. The good news is that it looks like the bullet went all the way through. Sorry," he added as Peter winced.

" 'Sokay," Peter said. He looked at his old friend. "I haven't said thanks yet."

Aaron smiled. " 'Sokay."

Peter frowned, looking around the cabin as Aaron took care of his wound. "Say, where's Jennifer?"

"Akira has her."

Peter sighed, slumping back as Aaron finished his crude bandage job.

"We'll get her back," he said.

"You've got that right."

Travis brought the machine down next to the hut that contained the weapons and gunpowder.

"Take over the controls," he called back over to Aaron, "and hold her steady. Don't let Eckels get near them this time. I'm going out to cover Otomo."

"Right," Aaron called out. He looked back down at Peter and squeezed his shoulder. "Hang on and take it easy. It may get a little rough."

"Don't worry about me," Peter said with as much bravado as he could muster. He hurt badly and he knew that Aaron knew it. But they didn't have time to worry about him now.

Aaron made his way to the control panel and took the codriver's seat as Travis popped the door. The time-guide hit the ground first, rifle out and ready.

Otomo stood over Katsu's body and looked seriously at the rest of the group. He spoke slowly and emphatically and Mundo translated his words.

"As you all are my witnesses, know that I take the boy named Katsu as my son. I give him my name. Forever now he shall be known as Otomo Katsu. So shall his memorial tablet in the Shrine of the Stone read."

Otomo gently pried the sword from Katsu's fingers and hoisted the body over his shoulder. He followed Travis out the door.

It was still madness and confusion on the upper level of the temple mound. Most of the ordinary villagers had long since fled. A core of Gray Raven's men, all warriors of the Buzzard Cult, had rallied themselves. They stood in a knot on the far side of the temple mound, brandishing their weapons and trying to talk themselves into attacking the time travelers.

Several of the fiercer warriors started forward when they saw Travis hit the ground, but he pointed his rifle in their direction and they stopped in their tracks.

"Easy does it, boys," Travis called out. "You don't want to end up like your boss man there."

Travis moved forward until he was beside Gray Raven's body. A single shot had drilled him through the center of the chest. The priest still looked faintly surprised and disappointed. Travis carefully checked for a pulse, but there was none.

He leaned over, never taking his eyes off the knot of screaming warriors and scooped up the rifle Gray Raven had got from Eckels. He slung it over his shoulder.

"I'll be taking this with me," he informed the Hill Maker warriors.

They seemed even more angry, but knew better than to try anything.

Otomo had disappeared into the hut, carrying Katsu's body over one shoulder and the sword in his other hand. He came out a moment later, empty-handed, strolling slowly as if out on a Sunday afternoon walk.

Travis had backed toward the hovering time machine, keeping his weapon trained on the Hill Maker warriors. Otomo joined him at the door, but Travis grabbed his arm and pointed.

"Look, that's one of your people, isn't it?"

The samurai who had been a Hill Maker captive lay midway between the time machine and knot of warriors. He was either dead or unconscious. They couldn't tell which from where they stood.

Otomo looked at Travis and nodded. He started after the body with his peculiar striding, strutting gait. He moved as slowly and as surely as if he'd just seen an interesting bunch of flowers that he wanted a closer look at.

One of the Hill Maker warriors stepped out of the group and aimed a drawn arrow at Otomo. He shouted something and fired. Otomo didn't even dodge. He snatched the arrow from the air before it could strike him, broke it, and contemptuously threw it to the ground. He checked the samurai, who seemed to have been knocked out in the wild melee. Carrying him in his arms like a baby, Otomo brought him back to the time machine.

Travis shook his head.

"I know you can't understand me, but, man, you have some style."

Otomo grunted and handed the man up to Mundo, who laid him on the floor beside Peter. Otomo pulled himself up into the craft and Travis followed.

The only villagers on the mound's upper level were Buzzard Warriors. The other captives had disappeared during the melee. Most of the ordinary villagers had vanished to the safety of their huts below.

Otomo spoke in his usual laconic manner and Mundo's eyes grew wide.

"Travis, better get us out of here. Otomo put a lighted fuse in a gunpowder keg—"

"Good Lord!" Travis cried as he dived for the controls. He grabbed the stick and jammed on the thruster. The craft shot away from the top of the mound.

"—and it should go off any second—"

Mundo was interrupted by a tremendous explosion that caught and rocked the time machine, tossing everyone like a handful of jumping beans. Travis grimly fought the controls, bringing them up out of the dive into which they'd been buffeted.

"—now," Mundo finally finished.

Travis put the machine in a slow loop back to the temple mound. Everyone who was able to crowded in close to get a look out of the front viewscreen.

"Wow," Aaron breathed.

Half the mound's top level was gone. It looked like a giant had reached out with an enormous ice-cream scoop and taken enough earth for a tremendous double-dipper. Some of the Buzzard Warriors had made a run for the hut when the time machine had lifted off. They had been caught in the blast. Like the hut itself, they too were now missing. The more prudent warriors had jumped to safety before the explosion.

Aaron sat back in his seat and sighed. He was desperately tired and sore, and some of the others were in a lot worse shape than he. But they weren't finished yet.

"Take us back to the village," he ordered Travis. "Now things are really going to get tough."

20

Time Storm

Aaron, Mundo, and Otomo stood before the closed gates of the Nipponjin village. Otomo had his hands on his hips and was looking with displeasure at the sentries, who were timidly peering at them over the wooden palisade. Aaron had a rifle slung over his shoulder. It was an uncomfortable weight to carry. He wished Travis could be with them, but someone had to mind the time machine, watch over Peter, and keep an eye on Eckels.

"We can't open the gate," a sentry explained haltingly to his captain. "Lord Akira has ordered them closed to you."

"Then bring Akira here," Otomo said, deliberately omitting the honorific. "There is much we have to discuss."

One of the guards scurried to obey.

"How do we know that Akira just won't have us shot out of hand?" Mundo asked nervously.

Otomo shrugged. "There's always that chance. It wouldn't be an honorable thing to do, but Akira has proved himself not to be an honorable man."

It took a few moments, but then Akira finally peered cautiously over the top of the palisade.

"Ah, Captain Otomo. And where have you been?"

"The village of the Hill Makers," Otomo replied frankly, "where we had to rescue one of our guests, who was specifically under my protection."

"How remarkable," Akira said weakly.

"It's more remarkable that he was there at all. Can you offer an explanation?"

"I?" Akira drew back affronted. "Why should I concern myself with the wanderings of a *gaijin* traveler?"

"Do you concern yourself with the equally odd travels of our own munitions?"

"What?"

"Somehow the Hill Makers obtained a quantity of guns, powder, and ammunition. A quantity sufficient to take the top off their temple when it blew up."

"How remarkable," Akira repeated.

"Yes," Otomo said coldly. He looked at Aaron, who was listening to Mundo's hurried translation of the conversation between the samurai captain and his lord. "Our guests have begged to take their leave. They have settled their differences and decided upon the ownership of the Steel Turtle. Eckels has admitted that it belonged to Travis, so in the interests of justice I rescinded your confiscation order. They are waiting at the Shrine of the Stone. I told them that I would bring Jennifer-san and the dragon."

Akira stared at them for long moments after Otomo had finished speaking. Aaron could see that he was trying desperately to control his anger and come up with something to confound their plans.

"You acted properly," Akira finally said. "But we can't let our guests leave without saying farewell. I shall bring Jennifer-san and the dragon to the shrine personally for a proper send-off. That is all."

He waited a long moment after dismissing Otomo, but the captain refused to bow to him. Aaron, following Otomo's cue, didn't bow either. Akira finally realized that they wouldn't extend their respects. He turned and stomped away angrily.

Otomo looked seriously at Aaron.

"You know," he said through Mundo, "we can't trust Akira. He'll surround himself with a party of men personally loyal to him and doubtless try to seize the Steel Turtle."

Aaron nodded. "But we had to get him to bring Jennifer and SStragh out of the village and into the open. That's the only hope we have to rescue them."

"A hope," Otomo said as they headed for the trail to the Shrine of the Stone. "But a faint one is all it is."

"Can you smell the air?" SStragh asked Jennifer.

She nodded. "I thought it was my imagination. I *hoped* that it was my imagination. But I guess not if you noticed it too."

She looked at the sky. It was a glorious late summer morning. The sun shone like clear gold. The sky was ocean blue, with a few wisps of clouds that looked like foaming whitecaps.

But there was a taste of bitter ozone lurking in the air and unaccountable shadows followed them as they made their way through the forest trail toward the Shrine of the Stone. The aura of subtle menace that SStragh and Jennifer could both detect in the air seemed a suitable accompaniment to Akira's entourage, which was also not quite what it appeared to be.

Everyone was on foot, except Akira, who rode in the lead on a gorgeously caparisoned horse, whose trappings matched the coloring of his brilliantly dyed kimono.

A squad of armed and armored samurai followed their lord, marching in double files ten men deep. The two men in the lead carried rising sun banners that billowed luxuriantly on the warm summer breeze. The others all had similar, but smaller, flags fluttering on short batons snugged into sockets on the back plates of their armor.

Then came SStragh and Jennifer, surrounded by a phalanx of another dozen samurai as an ostensible honor guard. But the time travelers knew better. The samurai weren't an honor guard. They were a guard, period.

Akira had come to the garden and told them that he was accompanying them to the Shrine of the Stone to say good-bye, but not even SStragh, a relative stranger to human expression, believed him. They both knew he was lying. They both knew that he had something up his sleeve, but they also knew that they were powerless to do anything to stop him. All they could do was go along and hope for an opportunity to escape.

Akira was taking no chances. The guard surrounded them the instant they left the citadel, even before they marched out of the village. A mouse couldn't have escaped from the formation. Jennifer and SStragh certainly couldn't.

The sky darkened as they entered the forest. Whether that was an effect of the sunlight filtering through the leaves of the overarching trees or a real change of atmospheric conditions, Jennifer couldn't tell.

But she was afraid that she could feel the electricity of a gathering storm.

The wreckage strewn around the Shrine of the Stone had been cleared away. All signs of death and violence had been removed, but the hole punched in the wall by Eckels and the time machine hadn't yet been repaired.

It was a grim reminder in this tranquil place of the violence that had shattered the peace of the forest just two days past.

The time machine stood in front of the shrine. Grim in the dappled shadow, it looked like some mythical monster that could devour them all. All its doors were shut. Its front viewscreen had been opaqued. Its power had been turned off. It crouched silent and immobile, more menacing than a snarling beast.

Aaron and Otomo stood before it. Aaron looked like he wanted to run to Jennifer, but somehow he restrained himself. Jennifer knew how he felt. She wanted to run to him, too.

The two were unarmed, except for the short sword sheathed at Otomo's side. He was missing his *katana*, his long sword. Jennifer wondered briefly what had happened to it, then her mind turned to more important things.

Did they trust Akira enough so that they appeared before him unarmed? If so, that was a mistake. A bad mistake.

"Greetings," Lord Akira said from atop his stallion. He looked around the clearing. "Where are the rest of our esteemed travelers?"

"They were hurt when we rescued Peter-san from the Hill Makers," Otomo said. "Mundo is attending them in the Steel Turtle."

Jennifer felt her heart skip. Travis, Peter, Katsu, even Eckels. Were they all hurt? How badly? Or was this some kind of scheme cooked up by Aaron and Otomo? She quickly told SStragh what was transpiring, but the dinosaur had no comment. She seemed content to wait and see what would happen.

"I would like to see them to express my personal wishes for a safe journey," Akira said.

"Doubtless," Otomo said. "First, however, it would do them immeasurable good to see Jennifer-san and the dragon again."

"I'm afraid that is impossible," Akira said flatly.

"I see." Otomo looked at Aaron. Though no words passed between them, it seemed that an understanding did. "In that case, I regret to tell you that I have lied to you."

"Lied?" Akira demanded, outraged. "In what way?"

Otomo drew the second sword that all samurai carried, the short sword called the *wakizashi*. It glittered in the dappled forest sunlight as he held it naked by his side.

"Travis-san isn't injured," Otomo said grimly. "He's not in the Steel Turtle. He's in the forest, sitting in the crotch of a tree. His arquebus is aimed at your head. He's an expert shot. He'll blow your head from your body if you don't release Jennifer-san and the dragon."

"Your conduct is outrageous! I order you to commit *seppuku* when this affair is over."

Otomo nodded. "As is your right, Lord."

Otomo's voice, Otomo's eyes, were implacable. But Jennifer suppressed a shiver when she heard Akira's bitter words. *Seppuku* was ritualized suicide that disgraced samurai were forced to perform in which they slashed open their own abdomens. Otomo, in helping them escape, was sentencing himself to a painful death. And he knew—and accepted—it.

"Aaron," she called out, "we can't let this happen."

Aaron looked at Otomo uncertainly when Jennifer told him what had just transpired. It was evident that whatever understanding Aaron and Otomo had, *seppuku* wasn't part of it. Aaron started to speak, stopped, shook his head. It looked like he made a difficult decision.

"We'll worry about that later," he shouted. "Come on through. We can't do anything with you in Akira's hands."

Jennifer started to argue, then realized that Aaron was right. She and SStragh had to get out of Akira's power. Otomo's actions had already condemned him to *seppuku*. But maybe she and SStragh could do something about that when they were free.

She started to push through the phalanx of guards. One of them grabbed for her arm, but she pushed his hand away.

"Lord Akira!" she called.

He turned in his saddle and glared at her. He spoke to his men, but never took his eyes off her and SStragh.

"Let them go, fool!"

The samurai parted ranks and Jennifer ran to Aaron, SStragh loping slowly at her side. She hugged Aaron fiercely, then noticed the bloodstained bandage on his upper arm.

"You're hurt!" she exclaimed.

"Not too badly," Aaron said.

"What about the others?"

"Peter's hurt, too," Aaron told her. "Worse than me, but I think he'll be all right. The medical kit in the time machine took care of him." Aaron paused. "And Katsu . . ."

He fell silent, unable or unwilling to continue.

Jennifer felt a cold chill pass through her, and she knew without being told.

"Dead?" she asked in a husky voice.

Aaron nodded, blinking rapidly.

Jennifer choked back tears herself. There was no time for tears now. Later, when everyone was safe, when it was quiet and peaceful and they had time to reflect on their adventure, she would think of the smiling, eager boy who had been more friend than servant. Later she could afford to cry.

Now she slipped her arm around Aaron's waist and turned to stare at Akira.

"What now?" she asked.

"I was hoping you'd think of something," Aaron admitted. "We could run for it . . . but Otomo . . ."

Jennifer nodded vehemently.

"We won't leave him behind to die."

"He won't come with us," Aaron said. "I already discussed that possibility with him. This is his world. He wants to stay here. Besides, his sense of honor won't allow him to run."

"He has too much honor for his own good."

"I could give Travis the signal," Aaron said hesitantly. "And that would be the end of Akira."

"We can't kill him in cold blood," Jennifer said flatly. "That would be too much like Eckels, or Akira himself."

"You're right," Aaron admitted. "It was just a possibility."

"Standoff," Jennifer said.

Aaron nodded.

Jennifer took a deep, desperate breath. There had to be something that could break the stalemate.

SStragh laid a clawed hand gently on Jennifer's shoulder.

"Jhenini—something is happening. The air smells of an approaching storm."

"You're right," Jennifer said. She'd been so wrapped up in their immediate problem that she hadn't noticed the steadily increasing indications of a coming time storm.

"What is it?" Aaron asked.

Jennifer pointed at the sky where, through the filter of tree branches, they could see lightning flash through suddenly angry-looking clouds.

"Time storm," Jennifer said. "One hit right before we used the Floating Stone in SStragh's valley on the dinosaur world. I think maybe they build up right before someone activates the temporal roadway. Maybe they dissipate the energy that's running between the ruptured timelines you told me about. You'd better call Travis in. Anything can happen when one of these things hit. Literally anything."

"But—"

"Do it," Jennifer said urgently. "Trust me."

Aaron nodded decisively. He pointed straight up with his right hand, forefinger extended. There was no indication that Travis had seen the signal, but a moment later he was simply standing beside them, rifle in his hand. Jennifer had never even heard him approach.

"All set?" he asked.

"Not quite," Aaron replied, and everything suddenly exploded around them.

The biggest bolt of lightning in the world screamed down from the sky and hit the roof of the Shrine of the Stone. The wooden building exploded as though someone had set off a dynamite charge within it.

The concussion threw Aaron and Jennifer to the ground. Instinctively he covered her body with his as fragments of boards showered down all around them.

Akira's horse screamed in fright and reared. Akira clung to its mane desperately. The ranks of samurai rippled, made an abortive motion to break and run, but Otomo's shouted command nailed them into place.

"What in heaven—" Travis began and the landscape around them went mad.

The forest disappeared. They were standing near a vast, endless cliff that seemed to float in a sea of mist. They were so close that two steps would put them in a different world. The miasma of muck and decay mixed in the air with the stench of ozone.

It was an opening to the pterodactyl world. The intelligent creatures swooped by the dozens, gliding high on the wild wind currents of their harsh planet. Akira called out in wonder at the sight of them. His horse staggered forward.

"Stop him!" Jennifer screamed. "The doors stay open for only a few moments!"

Otomo ran toward his lord, but it was too late. The horse, maddened and confused by the tumult, reared again, bucking and pawing at the sky as it was ripped apart by another explosion of lightning and thunder. Hail the size of oranges splattered on the ground. Steaming rain fell like a deluge.

This time Akira couldn't hang on. He pitched forward over the horse's neck and landed in a heap in the pterodactyl world. He reached out beseechingly. Otomo threw himself at Akira, but the storm had moved on.

The door, open so briefly, closed.

Others opened as the storm moved down the valley, drifting on the currents and eddies of the time winds. They saw quick snapshots of deserts, mountains, oceans, and what looked like lunar valleys. Some had buildings in them, some had people, some had nothing. Some were as familiar as pictures in history books, others were weird scenes out of a fever-maddened imagination.

Aaron and Jennifer ran to Otomo, who was staring at the spot, now looking perfectly normal, where Akira had disappeared.

"He's gone," Otomo said, rain streaming down upon his face.

Jennifer gripped his arm.

"You must forget about *seppuku*," she told him. "Honor requires that you stay alive to lead your village. There's no one else to do it."

Otomo nodded, his expression distant.

"You're right," he said. "At least until we discover the *daimyo*'s desires."

"Good luck, Otomo-san," Aaron said.

Otomo turned and looked at Aaron and Jennifer.

"It has been . . . extraordinary . . . friends."

Aaron and Jennifer bowed. Otomo, allowing himself a small smile, returned their bow a precise millimeter.

"Let's get out of here," Aaron called as they went back to Travis.

The rain had already let up in this part of the valley, but they were soaked to the skin and shivering in air that was suddenly, unnaturally cool.

"All right," Travis said. He lifted a hand in salute to Otomo, who was watching them impassively while the other samurai milled about uncertainly.

"Wait," Otomo called.

They didn't understand his words, but his tone made them stop. The samurai turned to one of his men and snapped an order. The man handed Otomo his sheathed *katana*, his long sword.

Otomo turned to Aaron, holding it out to him.

"This is for you," he said. "You have proved to be a leader. You are worthy of it."

Aaron looked at Jennifer, who translated Otomo's words.

"Thank you," he said to the samurai. "*Domo arigato*."

Otomo permitted himself another smile, then turned and shouted at his men. They marched off in formation back to their village. Aaron knew that they were moving out of his life, that he'd never see them again. He wished them well, but most of all he wished them and the Hill Makers peace.

He turned toward the waiting time machine. As they neared, the door opened silently.

"Pull up to the fragment of roadway," Travis ordered Mundo, who sat at the controls. "We'd better clear some of the debris away from it before we try to get out of here."

Travis, Aaron, Jennifer, and SStragh all started to move aside pieces of the shattered shrine. Travis suddenly stopped, stooped over, and stared at the base of the Floating Stone.

"Well I'll be—" he said.

"What is it?" Aaron asked.

"Look."

Travis pointed at a gleam of shiny metal embedded in an edge of the black roadway.

"What is it?" Jennifer asked.

"It looks like a part of the temporal mechanism that controls the time fields," Travis said. "I wonder . . ."

"What?" Aaron prompted.

Travis looked up eagerly.

"This is what's causing the temporal rifts. The paradox explosion tore the temporal control mechanism apart. Pieces of the mechanism were scattered with bits of roadway through time and space. These mechanisms rooted themselves in whatever timestream they ended up in."

"Putting the pieces in activated the roadway we used to escape from the last world we were in," Aaron said. "Taking them out may deactivate this roadway and seal this rift."

"Maybe," Travis said with a grin. "There's only one way to find out for sure."

"Let's do it," Aaron said, grinning back.

Travis waved the time machine forward. It came up at a crawl and stopped right before the Floating Stone.

"You'd all better get in," Travis said. "We don't know exactly what'll happen when I detach the control fragment. No sense in it happening to all of us."

Aaron shook his head.

"I'm staying with you," he said. "There's a promise I have to fulfill."

"Me too," Jennifer said.

"Not this time," Aaron said. "You and SStragh are going into the machine."

He spoke with the sense of command that had lately come to him. Jennifer recognized it and knew that she wasn't going to change his mind this time. She nodded.

"Okay. Be careful." She kissed him quickly on the cheek, then turned and helped SStragh get into the time machine. The door hissed shut after them. The machine rumbled onto the Floating Stone. Aaron had already replaced the temporal circuitry he'd removed, just in case something had gone wrong during their confrontation with Akira. The machine disappeared.

Travis and Aaron looked at each other.

"We'd better move fast," Travis said. "We don't know how much time we'll have if this baby starts to shut down."

Aaron nodded. "Here goes nothing," he said.

Aaron stuck his sword in his belt, then together they reached down and tugged the control fragment from the roadway, at the same moment leaping on the Floating Stone. Instantaneously, before the cold wave of nausea could grip them, they saw a sparkling, opaque barrier erupt from the end of the roadway.

Aaron had a brief moment of exultation. He knew they'd closed off this world. He knew that they had found a way to repair the damage to the timestream. The vow he'd made in the memory of Grandpa Carl would not be in vain.

Then the frigid sickness of time travel overcame him—

21

Return to Dinosaur World

—and he was in another world.

The heat and humidity of the dinosaur world hit Aaron in the face like a slap from a wet towel.

He grabbed Travis's arm, a smile on his face. But the smile faded when he saw the time machine canted on its side, caught in a thick, elastic vine net, trapped like a puppy in a sack.

Travis and Aaron were surrounded by armed, grim-looking Mutata.

Aaron opened his mouth to say something, to call out that they were friends and meant no harm. But he had no time.

The Mutata charged.

DINOSAUR SAMURAI SKETCHBOOK

A Record of My Adventures by Aaron Cofield

Pages 222 and 223: Eckels' cave showed a combination of sophisticated planning and animal cunning.

Page 224: A time rift opened and threw Akira into the world of the Saorod.

Page 225: There it was—part of the temporal control mechanism, imbedded in a segment of the pathway.

Pages 226 and 227: Jen and Sstragh saw Eckels drive the time machine into a timestorm.

Page 228: A portrait of Gray Raven.

Page 229: The hill-maker cultists captured Peter, but not without a fight.

Pages 230 and 231: There was Captain Otomo, a samurai warrior through training and breeding, with his troops.

Page 232: It was a tense moment as the rampaging Gairk crashed to the ground at my feet.

Page 233: The timestorms provided all kinds of dangers, like the Saorod that emerged from one and saw Jennifer alone.

Page 234: Samurai warriors became prisoners of the hill-makers.

Page 235: Then there was the buzzard cult, which summoned its worshippers with a conch call at dawn.

Page 236: Danger lurked at every turn. Here Peter unexpectedly ran into a pair of Gairk.

MAIN ENTRANCE

CUTAWAY DIAGRAM OF
ECKELS' CAVE

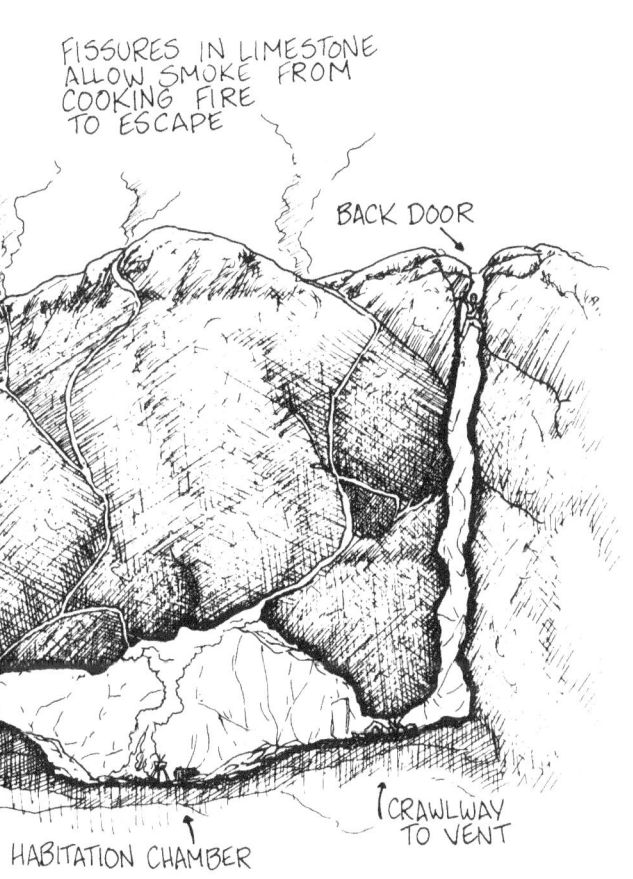

FISSURES IN LIMESTONE
ALLOW SMOKE FROM
COOKING FIRE
TO ESCAPE

BACK DOOR

HABITATION CHAMBER

CRAWLWAY
TO VENT

AKIRA IS THROWN INTO THE
SAOROD WORLD THROUGH
THE TIME-RIFT...

TEMPORAL CONTROL
MECHANISM
FRAGMENT IMBEDDED
IN SHATTERED
PATHWAY SEGMENT...

JEN AND SSTRAGH WATCH
ECKELS DRIVE THE TIME
MACHINE AT THE FLOATING
STONE, AS THE
TIMESTORM BREAKS...

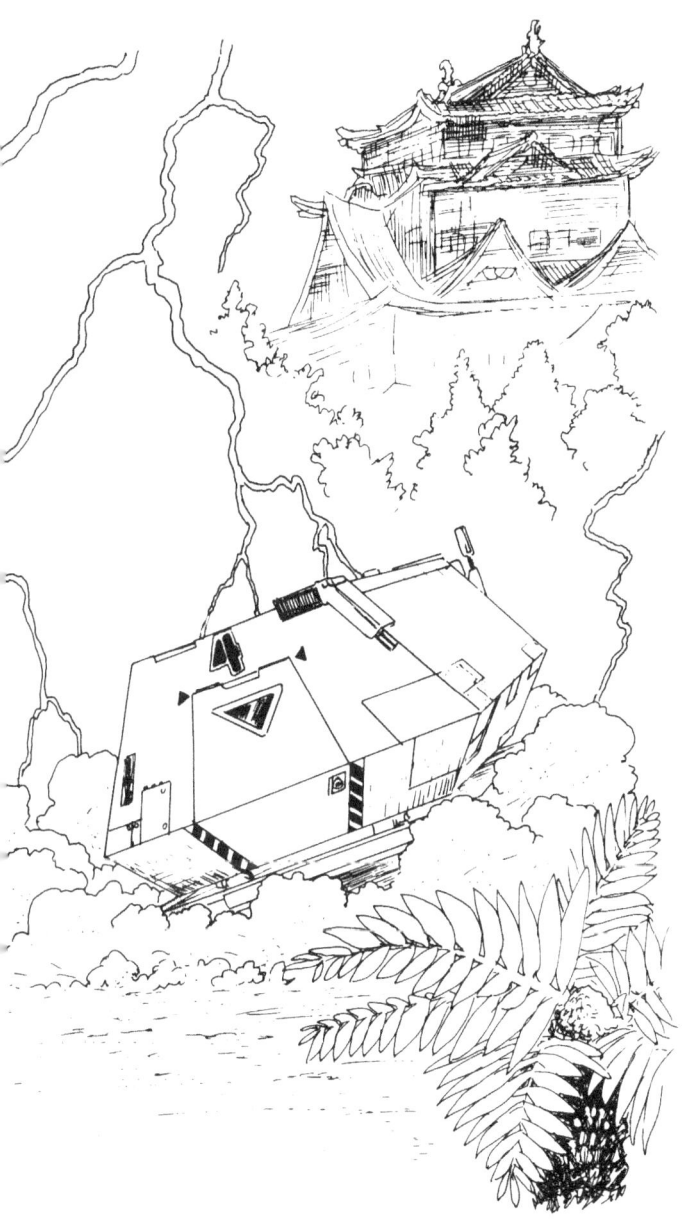

GRAY RAVEN

PETER FOUGHT TO
ESCAPE HIS CAPTORS,
THE HILL-MAKER
CULTISTS...

CAPTAIN OTOMO AND HIS MEN...

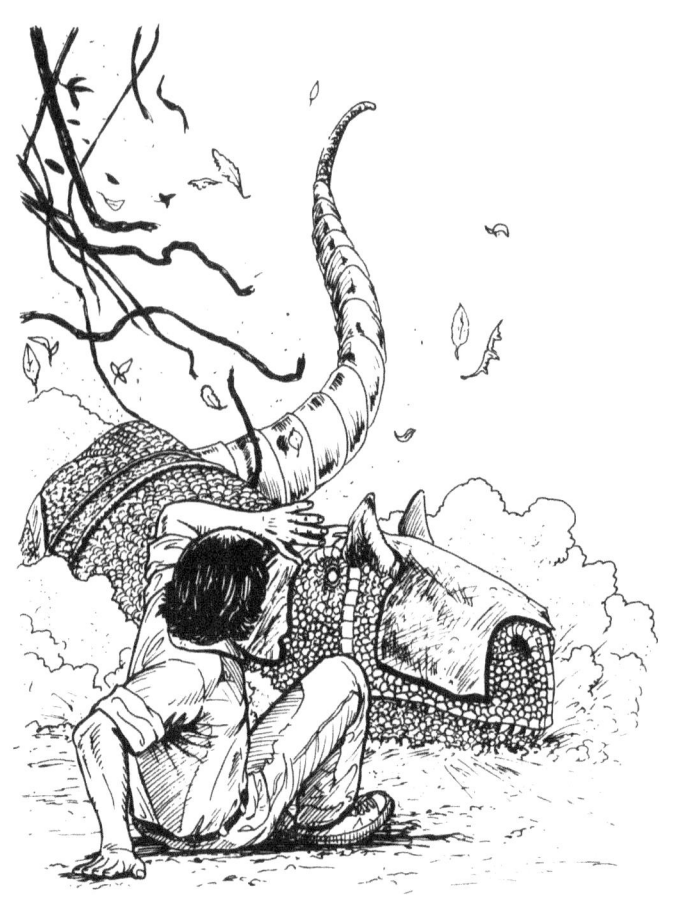

THE GAIRK CRASHED TO THE GROUND
RIGHT AT MY FEET...

THE SAOROD FLEW
OUT OF THE TIME-
STORM AND SWOOPED
DOWN ON JENNIFER...

PRISONERS OF THE HILL-MAKERS

PETER ENCOUNTERS
A PAIR OF GAIRK
ON THE TRAIL...

Glossary of Mutata Terms

The Sounds of the Mutata

The sounds made by the Mutata (a race of sentient dinosaurs most similar to the duckbills of our pre-history) are produced through their long nasal horns. In the novels, they are omitted for the most part. However, the most common sounds are a nasal bleet, a snort, a full roar, and a trill.

Pronunciation Key

The Mutata language has been transcribed into an approximation of phonetic English. Most consonants are pronounced as they would be pronounced in that language. In most cases, "a" is pronounced as the 'a' in cat; "e" as the 'e' in met; "i" as the 'i' in dim (though an ending "i" is pronounced as the 'ee' in meet); "o" as the 'o' in solo; "u" as the 'oo' in moot; "ai" as 'i' in ride; "ei" as the 'ea' in heaven; "ah" as the 'a' in tall. Some of the Mutata sounds cannot be adequately reproduced by the human larynx. In those cases, the closest English sound has been used, as in "jh", which for the Mutata is glottal stop much like a very rapid "jeh-eh", the last syllable being a quick aspirant. In some cases, a literal translation of the Mutata word has been substituted, as in "Speaker" or "Giving." There are also subtle posture and scent aspects to the Mutata language which, unfortunately, must be lost in the written form and which humans can never imitate. Any human must always be partially mute and deaf to the Mutata language as spoken by the dinosaurs.

aii   An imperative: to be performed immediately.

Baosiot   Unintelligent predatory dinosaurs—the allosaurus, possibly.

bhieye   "Thank you."

broaii   The Gairk war club, a massive wooden mallet tipped with several protruding blades of obsidian. The Gairk will usually carry two, one for the right hand, one for the left. Like the Mutata, the left hand is used when striking another sentient creature; the right is for "non-intelligent" lifeforms.

chodoe	"Follow me." An imperative, used only by a superior Mutata to his or her social inferiors.
ciosie	A demand for satisfaction. Ciosie means literally "The decision of the All-Ancestor"—in other words, letting the right or wrong of an issue be decided by combat, with the All-Ancestor's influence supposedly determining the outcome.
daii soo	Literally, "Pause (or wait) several breaths."
ehei	To go outside a dwelling. Also, to wander.
Eikels	Eckels.
Floraria	Unintelligent predatory dinosaurs, possibly the Tyrannosaurus family.
gaedo	An affirmative given by a younger to an elder. "Yes."
Gairk	The racial name for a species of sentient, small allosaurs.
geedo	"Yes." As spoken by peers.
geiree	"Come here," or "Approach me." An imperative form.
gheodo	Literally, "I cannot do that," with the added emphasis that the refusal is based on a superior's orders.
Giving	Translation of the Mutata phrase meaning "The time when the spirit is given to the All-Ancestor." The funeral rite for Mutata.

jhaka

The village in which Mutata live, each under the rule of its own OColi.

Jhenini

Jenny.

jhiehai

Scavenger proto-birds—these are deliberately enticed to feed on the bodies of dead Mutata.

khiisoo

A demand for obedience: "You must obey!"

LongDay

Or oGhielas. The summer solstice. As with almost all human cultures, the Mutata and Gairk also mark the solstices for religious celebration and ceremony.

Mutata

The racial name for Sstragh's species of sentient dinosaurs.

niijeks

Mouse-like rodents which feed on the stored grains within the Mutata encampments.

OColi

Literally, the Eldest. The ruler of a particular Mutata tribe is nearly always the oldest among them. Can be either male or female, though the males generally live the longest.

OColihi

The Ancient Path. The code of ethics and behavior which govern the Mutata. This code is handed down via a verbal tradition through the OTsio. The beginnings of the ritualized OColihi are lost in the long centuries of the Mutata past.

oei | A modifier. When used in conjunction with other words, it indicates "many" or "a large amount."

OTsio | Teacher. Each youngling Mutata, when the tribe has returned from the first Nesting Walk after their hatching, is assigned an OTsio to guide their development. The OTsio becomes a parent-analogue, though a Mutata of that age is considered independent.

otsioiue | The OTsio's student.

Raajek | Sstragh's OTsio, and a proponent of the OChiihi, or New Path—a mindset at variance with the old ways of Mutata behavior.

saorod | A species of pterosaur in Dinosaur World, with about a 3-inch wingspan.

Speaker | Translation of the Mutata title-phrase meaning "One who speaks the words of the Eldest."

tiafer | The original name of the current OColi.

werada | A death caused by a Mutata—specifically, the left-handed type of killing, not the right-handed killing that would be done to an animal.

werata | Pain.

whiaso | A "right-handed" killing, or the killing of a simple, unintelligent creature.

yeie   A modifier, indicating a negative:
                            "I will not" or "This is not so."
                            Also used as a quick denial: "No!"

zhiotae   The Gairk "Readers of Omens" or
                            shaman. Functions as an advisor to
                            the Gairk OColi in spiritual mat-
                            ters. The Mutata have no ana-
                            logue occupation.

We want to hear from readers!

Your opinion of the Dinosaur World series is important to us. We welcome all feedback about the series.

Write or email to the editors at the following address:

J. T. Colby & Company, Inc.
Purveyors of Time Travel Instruments and Accessories™

Manhanset House
Dering Harbor, New York 11965-0342
bricktower@aol.com
bricktowerpress.com

RAY BRADBURY, one of the greatest writers of fantasy and horror fiction in the world today, has published some 500 short stories, novels, plays, and poems since his first story appeared in *Weird Tales* when he was twenty years old. Among his many famous works are *Fahrenheit 451, The Illustrated Man,* and *The Martian Chronicles.* He has also written the screenplays for *It Came from Outer Space, Something Wicked This Way Comes,* and *Moby Dick.* Mr. Bradbury was Idea Consultant for the United States Pavilion at the 1964 World's Fair, has written the basic scenario for the interior of Spaceship Earth at EPCOT, Disney World, and is doing consultant work on city engineering and rapid transit. When one of the Apollo Astronaut teams landed on the moon, they named Dandelion Crater there to honor Mr. Bradbury's novel, *Dandelion Wine.* Recently Mr. Bradbury flew in an airplane for the first time.

STEPHEN LEIGH is the author of several science fiction novels, including *Crystal Memory, The Bones of God,* and the best-selling *Alien Tongue.* He is also a contributing author to the Hugo-nominated *Wild Cards* shared-world series. Currently Mr. Leigh lives in Ohio.

JOHN J. MILLER has written four novels and a number of short stories, including ten in the *Wild Cards* shared-world series. His nonfiction has appeared in magazines as diverse as *Tropical Fish Hobbyist* and *Baseball Digest.* He resides in Albuquerque, New Mexico.